BOOK ONE
NIGHTMARES
PROPHETIC

BRANDON PETRYNA

iUniverse, Inc.
Bloomington

Prophetic
Nightmares Book One

Copyright © 2012 by Brandon Petryna

All rights reserved. No part of this book may be used or reproduced by any means, graphic, electronic, or mechanical, including photocopying, recording, taping or by any information storage retrieval system without the written permission of the publisher except in the case of brief quotations embodied in critical articles and reviews.

This is a work of fiction. All of the characters, names, incidents, organizations, and dialogue in this novel are either the products of the author's imagination or are used fictitiously.

Vanessa Billedeau, editor

iUniverse books may be ordered through booksellers or by contacting:

iUniverse
1663 Liberty Drive
Bloomington, IN 47403
www.iuniverse.com
1-800-Authors (1-800-288-4677)

Because of the dynamic nature of the Internet, any web addresses or links contained in this book may have changed since publication and may no longer be valid. The views expressed in this work are solely those of the author and do not necessarily reflect the views of the publisher, and the publisher hereby disclaims any responsibility for them.

Any people depicted in stock imagery provided by Thinkstock are models, and such images are being used for illustrative purposes only.

Certain stock imagery © Thinkstock.

ISBN: 978-1-4759-2017-8 (sc)
ISBN: 978-1-4759-2019-2 (hc)
ISBN: 978-1-4759-2018-5 (e)

Printed in the United States of America

iUniverse rev. date: 05/04/2012

For my mother

Acknowledgments

◊ ◊ ◊

There are a lot of people I wish to thank. First off, there's my mother, Mémés, Madison, Sally and Tamara. Thank you all for the input and the time it took to review my first drafts. I hope you guys enjoy what has become of that, at one time, 50 paged project. I also want to thank my friends for being extremely supportive: your enthusiasm gave me that extra boost. To my good friend George: thanks for the time you took to work with me. I know I can be a pain and I am grateful that you stuck by my side. So many people have been there for me during this project: friends, family and even great teachers: Michelle, your opinion has always mattered to me. Thank you for being part of this project. Lindsay, you're a great evaluator and I'm happy that you played a role in the making of *Prophetic*. Anne, my mentor, you of all people have been there the longest. Thank you for working with me even before this class project became an actual published book. And equal thanks go to Joel for keeping me on track during the first draft. I should also thank my brothers Kaige and Konnor simply for being there and thinking that the idea of me writing a book was "cool". Finally, I thank the person who, without her help, *Prophetic* wouldn't be what it is today: Vanessa, you are the greatest editor out there and I can't begin to express how thankful I am to have teamed up with you. Without your help, my audience would have probably seen what a story really looks like when the author does their own edits. Oh and by the way, I suppose "arm's length" does have a nice ring to it: thanks Papas.

BP

"*Life can either be accepted or changed. If it is not accepted, it must be changed. If it cannot be changed, then it must be accepted.*"

~ Unknown author

Riley's First Encounter

◊ ◊ ◊

Riley stood alone in the forest. She could not remember how she got there. She could narrowly see the beast coming for her, and it sent chills down her spine. Her eyes flickered in every direction. *Where are you?* A rustling came from the bushes. Her heart had never beaten so hard.

A dark wheezing voice called her name. As she stumbled backward, a sudden silence fell. The creature had come forward, revealing itself. It hovered a foot from the ground and wore a black cloak that covered its face. Bellow the cloak dangled two rough-looking, birdlike feet. Encased in terror, Riley wondered what it was.

The creature lifted a long, pale green finger at her which swayed left and right. The finger was then raised up toward the hooded face and followed by a long, wheezing hush. Riley reached for her pockets. "Stay back!" she shouted. Whatever it was she was looking for, it was not there. "I can still kill you!" she lied, as worry spread through her veins.

"Let me in!" the creature commanded. Everything faded to black.

Chapter 1

◊ ◊ ◊

Riley's head shot up from her pillow. "Not again!" she cried out. Her fair hair fell into her face as she drowned herself in her tear- and sweat-filled hands. "Why does this keep happening?" she cried.

Dawn crept through the window, casting a hauntingly grey glow throughout the room. She forced herself out of bed. Tears slipped gently down her cheeks as she stepped over the piles of clean and dirty laundry stretched across the bedroom. She headed toward the kitchen through the hallway. A plain, pale blue paint coated every wall in the lonely bungalow. A few old family photos hung in the hallways, most of which featured two very fair, blue-eyed children and a man who was undoubtedly their father as they resembled him nearly identically with the exception of their thin eyelashes – a trait inherited from their professional-looking mother.

Riley took a seat at her kitchen table where a large, black digital camera had been laid lifeless, tempting her to pick it up and capture the world. Her racing heart urged her otherwise. Besides, her world in Fallsdale was not worth photographing: the sky was covered in dark clouds each night and day, the trees and flowers had already lost their colour and beauty, despite the fact August had not yet come to an end, and above all, the murders and freak accidents that were slowly creeping into the tri-city area pointed to the fact that the world was going to hell.

The coffee maker dinged. Riley sleeked her blonde bangs behind her ear and walked across the small kitchen to pour herself a cup. Just above the sink sat a rectangular window that gave her a view of the dark clouds hovering over top of the black trees and withering grass. The silhouette made her father's profile appear in her thoughts, and a shudder escaped her lips. They were great big clouds of smoke: *dangerous, murderous clouds*, she thought.

The phone suddenly rang, making Riley drop her mug of coffee onto the ceramic tiles. "Hell!" she screamed as she looked at the broken cup and cracked flooring. She stomped over to the phone that hung on the wall by the wooden table. "Hello?" she answered, but only static hissed. Furious, she slammed the cordless back onto its charger and stomped back over to the sink. She grabbed napkins off the countertop to clean the broken mug off the floor.

She was fuming with anger. On all fours, she crouched, cleaning up the mess. *Get a hold of yourself Riles; they're only dreams.* A little black fly buzzed passed her head and settled down on the white cupboard door beneath the sink. SMACK. She tried to hit the bug, but it was too quick, and it managed to buzz off before she could kill it. She hated the pest. It had been a month now that she had been trying to kill it but had failed at every attempt.

With every passing night, an irrepressible terror fell upon Riley during sleep. She experienced continuous nightmares of a cloaked creature murdering unrecognizable people. Each dream had played out a different scenario for the past few weeks. One was of a man walking in a dark alley, when out of the shadows came the beast with the cloak and talons. It was only yesterday when Riley had noticed that the setting in her dream was the alley by the old bowling center in downtown Fallsdale. On top of that, she could have sworn that she was now able to picture the stranger even more clearly than before. She recalled another dream where a man and a little girl were also murdered. This dream she figured to have been in Fredsfurd by the pizzeria. All of her night terrors made more sense as time paced on. The blurred figures of men and women took tangible, recognizable forms, and the places they died always seemed to be real places where Riley had once visited.

But what was probably the most peculiar happening of all was the sense Riley had of being watched. Her nerves made her shiver as she brushed her teeth after breakfast. She spit in the sink, swished some water in her mouth straight from the tap, spit it out, and cleaned up her splash marks on the mirror with a couple squares of toilet paper, which she then used to clean the toothpaste from the porcelain sink. The shivers caught her for the fortieth time since the nightmares began. Her eyes lifted to observe her own reflection, she did not feel right. Her hands were gripping the sink bowl when her eyes made an uncontrollable twitch to the right and found the reflection of something watching her – a sort of shadow-like being standing behind her. She spun on spot. It was gone. *Of course it wasn't real,* she told herself. *It was just my imagination.* She checked the hallway and kitchen, just to make sure. No one was around.

Riley was alone. Nevertheless, she stayed on her guard. This was her first two week vacation in ages, and she found herself spending it hiding out beneath the covers. "Pathetic," she sighed. As she thought of her wasted time spent hiding, she realized the terrors did not seem quite as frightening as she had thought. With that in mind, she went about her day vacuuming the floor, washing the sink full of dishes and cleaning the bathroom. Her bedroom could wait for another day. Feeling more relaxed and at peace, she headed to the living room to settle in and watch some television.

That night, she was able to fall asleep early with ease. However, in the sleeping world, her mind was vulnerable. She saw a man and woman running swiftly down a moonlit hill. And there it was: the cloaked creature. It burst from the cluster of trees at the top of the hill and raced down after its screaming victims. It was hovering off the ground. Those bird feet seemed useless. The creature caught up in an instant, and everything happened so quickly. The creature pierced its sharp, pale green claw into the man's back. The woman was pushed away by her helpless friend. She stumbled forward a few yards and fell to her hands and knees. The man froze, and the blood left his tanned face as he stared ahead into nothingness. Keeping hold on the man, the cloaked creature rose over him, turned, and pointed at the woman. "I'm coming for you," it said in a dark, bone-chilling voice. It then threw the man down on the dew-covered grass. Everything faded away, and Riley could feel herself waking.

The first breath coming back to reality made the pounding in her head disappear. She lay on her side. She must have been twisting and turning all night since the comforter had fallen off the bed. She stretched, pulled herself up, and crossed the messy bedroom toward the hallway leading into the kitchen.

She went straight for the fridge and pulled out a plate of cinnamon buns, which she heated in the microwave and ate with her morning coffee. There was a faint thud at the door. She instantly got off her chair to open the door and grab the Saturday paper resting at her feet. The door shut behind her as she stepped back into the house. She pulled the paper out of its blue plastic sac as the picture of a familiar man caught her eyes. Riley was perplexed. The paper told her that this familiar face was now dead. "Dead?" her voice quivered quietly. She was halfway down the main hall when she stopped motionless in her tracks. Her heart began to beat harder.

As her dream suddenly raced back to her, she realised that the man in the paper looked so much like the man from the bowling center in her nightmare. *It couldn't be him. Come on Riles, you're losing it*, she pleaded with herself.

There was a knock at the door. She dropped the paper on the wooden shoe rack by the closet and answered. To her surprise, there stood her mother. She was as professional-looking as ever. She wore a black dress, a coat, and a matching pair of shoes. Despite the surprise visit, Riley was most curious as to know why her mother seemed so happy; however, any sign of happiness from her mother would have sparked questions, anyhow. "Mom?" Riley could not help contain the confusion that spilled from her mouth in one single word. She had not been in contact with anyone in her family in ages, and even her older brother Jared had become a stranger.

Her mother held a white envelope in her giddy hands. "How have you been?" she asked through a smile of sparkling teeth.

"Uh, good," Riley replied, still processing this unfamiliar woman. "How are you?" she stammered.

"I'm very well and have the best news! Your brother is getting married!" exclaimed her mother as she clapped her hands together and began hopping on the spot.

"Married?" Riley repeated, smiling, "My brother? Which one?"

"The black one," answered her mother jokingly.

They both giggled. Her mother explained that she and Tim were excited about Craig's proposal and that they both loved the girl.

Riley's smile disappeared halfway through her mother's thought. If there was anyone who Riley had not spoken to in a while, it was Tim. She grew up hating him. He was never satisfied. He always had something to complain about and never seemed to smile. Riley often wondered what might have crawled up his butt to make him act as he did; however, whatever the reason for his immaturity and insolence, there was never a valid reason for him to be such an ignorant stepfather. Their relationship had become so bad that they had started arguing out in public. Riley could not remember a time when they had actually gotten along.

"So what do you think, Riles?" asked her mother.

Riley woke from her trance. "Sorry?" she said.

"Be a bridesmaid?"

"Um, yeah sure," she answered, but she did not understand why they would want her for bridesmaid. She did not know the woman her mother spoke about, and above all, she did not know anything about Craig being with a woman at all.

Her mother handed her the invitation, and they said their goodbyes. Liz then drove off in her black sedan and Riley headed to the living room where she sat on her blue couch and read the invite.

Mr. & Mrs. Wilfred White
request the pleasure of your company
at the marriage of their daughter
Parker White
to
Mr. Craig Jackson Wilson
at The Holy Cross Church, Fallsdale
on Saturday 17th October, 2004
at 14:30 O'Clock
and afterwards at
The AuClaire Hotel of Georgia
R.S.V.P. by September 1st

Riley stopped there. The rest of the note was a list of foods to choose from. She re-read the woman's name. *Who's Parker White?* She turned her head toward the living room window and watched rain beginning to tap against the glass. Riley took another glance at the invitation. She placed it on her coffee table, turned off the light, and lay down on the sofa. Her eyes were getting heavy, and she felt herself drifting away from her screwed up world.

Chapter 2

Whispers echoed from every direction. Riley rubbed her eyes and noticed that she was standing in the dark. Nothing was visible except a sparkling blue light piercing through the thick darkness. She walked toward the light where whispers seemed to come from. Her body felt numb. It was as if she was mindlessly being pulled toward the beautiful shimmering glow. She reached for it, and almost immediately, a pale white hand reached back for her as whispers began to call her name.

The thud of the weekend paper hitting the door woke her up. Sweat drops cooled on her forehead. She choked on her panting breath. Before she knew it, she was sitting up on the sofa, coughing. She cleared her throat and wiped her forehead. Her head was throbbing. She stood up and made her way to the front door. A quick glance around the neighborhood showed that it looked just as it had yesterday morning and every day before that: grey and lifeless. She grabbed the paper at her feet and walked back in.

Riley pinched the bridge of her nose. After a cup of water, the ache seemed to disappear, but the dream had gotten even clearer. The directory in her phone was the first place she went. After tossing the paper onto the table, she began to scroll through her contacts.

She looked up Dr. Rochelle, a psychiatrist in Fredsfurd, who she had found on the internet two weeks after her chronic nightmares began. The phone rang once before a young secretary answered in a cheery voice.

"Hi," Riley replied. "Listen, I was wondering—" Something stopped her in mid sentence: a voice. There was a pause before the woman on the other end of the call started talking.

"Hello?" asked the receptionist.

"Hello," whispered a boy.

"I'm sorry, I didn't get that," she said.

Almost in complete synchronization, this strange, childlike voice mimicked the secretary. "Hello?" she asked again.

"Hello?" he said.

"Um, one sec, I think I have a bad connection. I'll call you back." Riley hung up the phone almost immediately. She hit redial and waited with the silent phone pressed to her ear.

"Ring. Ring. Ring," chimed a boyish voice. Fear left her standing still and listening. "Riley?" the voice whispered. "Riley? Let me in."

She slammed the cordless back onto the charger and paced through the kitchen several times before her eyes fell on the picture of a bride and groom on the cover of the Fallsdale Star. Uneasiness set in. She contemplated calling Fallsdale's priest, Father Monsignor. *He won't be able to help, but it would make me feel better. He'll think I'm crazy. What if I am?* Worry dominated her mind, but what frightened her most was what she might find on the other end of that phone. She spoke words of comfort to herself in her head. *It was a bad connection. Don't worry. You heard wrong: no one actually said your name.* Before she knew it, her ear was pressed to the phone once again, listening and waiting for the voice. The only sound coming from the phone was the dial tone buzzing in her ear.

She dialed the number of the church and was greeted by a deep, royal voice after the third ring.

"Sir?" asked Riley hesitantly.

"Yes, how can I help you?" asked the man.

After hesitating, she briefly explained her night terrors, the man in the paper, the shadow in the hallway, and the boy on the phone. Riley claimed that they must have all been her imagination. All the while, the man seemed very calm and listened carefully. Riley was a little taken aback when he said, "I think we should meet." It seemed like he thought it was urgent. "Today perhaps?" he asked. Riley hesitated. She had not entered a church in years and had never confessed to a priest before. "Let's say around 5:30. We should speak privately about your sins," his voice shook gravely.

Do it, whispered the voice in the back of her head. "Uh, ok. If you think I should," she replied shamefully. She hung up the phone and leaned against the wall, feeling embarrassed. *What must he think of me?*

All was quiet. The pale grey light filtered through the dense sheet of clouds and peered through the living room window. Riley stared out the window from where she sat across the room on her dark blue couch. The silence grated on her nerves. *Am I going crazy?* Her life was now characterized by voices and visions. She had always been in full control of herself; however, she now could not possibly feel more afraid or vulnerable.

Leaning against the window, Riley watched the rain tap against the glass. As she looked out into the gloomy world, she overtaken by a feeling of unease once more – she was being watched. She shifted her body away from the window and walked toward the hallway. The thought of that shadowy silhouette kept appearing in her mind. All the lights in the house were out. The air felt cool, and the buzzing noise the fly made while zipping around the room kept getting louder.

She watched it circle up by the ceiling as she made her way into the kitchen. Her breath was shaky, and she used the table for support. Vapour from her breath formed in the cold air. She had been wrong – she was not just afraid – she was terrified. She breathed heavily, the stream of her white fog growing thicker. Silence fell. She quickly turned around. The now silent fly was an arm's length away from her face. It defused into tiny particles in the air and became a black smoke that slowly dispersed into the shape of the cloaked creature from her nightmares. She gasped as it continued to approach her from such a short distance. From beneath the cloak covering the creature's face, reached two long, sharp, pale green hands.

Riley abruptly sat up on the couch. Panting heavily and covered in sweat, she scanned the living room and realized it was just another dream.

◊ ◊ ◊

Later that afternoon, she paced back and forth in her kitchen while waiting for her appointment with the priest. She was tired. Her fingers kept brushing the sleep from her eyes. To make her exhaustion worse, she continuously worried about what Monsignor would think. She did try to keep a detailed note of every last unusual thing that had happened since the dreams began, but her story sounded completely insane. *It's because of the dreams.* She tried diagnosing herself, saying that the first nightmare had been so scary that she kept thinking about it before bed, and that was why the creature kept reappearing. That was why she had been hearing voices and seeing silhouettes of people running around. *It's just lack of sleep.*

Although her theory made sense, it still did not explain the man in the paper. From the back of her mind echoed the word *coincidence.* She tried convincing herself that her foresight of a man's death was just simply something natural like a reverse déjà vu. Her stomach churned; it was a monster that had murdered that man. This uneasiness made her decide to go through with her plans. For some strange reason beyond her entire being, she felt it was right to visit Father Monsignor. She worried that her lack of faith would complicate things. He would know that she did not attend church; everyone knows everyone in Fallsdale. She paced in fear. As she spun on foot toward the refrigerator, she noticed the fly on the light blue wall. She walked over to the insect. With one swift whack, the fly lay motionless in the palm of her hand. A strange shift took place in the air, and she felt anxious holding the fly in her hand. Although it had died, she was wary that it would turn into something supernatural as it had in her dream. She slowly turned her palm face down, dropping the bug. She backed away from it toward the kitchen table until her leg rubbed against a black wooden chair. *Maybe the priest is for the best.* She looked at the time on the oven clock. *If Monsignor doesn't work out, I'll just sum up the courage to call Rochelle.* Without a second glance at the fly on the floor, she stepped out of the kitchen and into the main hall.

Riley pulled out her black pea coat from the closet, put it on, and walked out the door. She opened the garage door and climbed into her silver sedan. She pulled out of her driveway, using the remote to close the garage door. Worries about her appointment flowed into her mind. She wanted to meet with the priest to secure a sense of safety, but she feared he would think she was insane.

Riley parked the car in the church parking lot and stepped out onto the cold cement. She walked over to the large oak doors that she still felt uncertain about entering. She reached for the handle, gasped when she found it was burning hot, and quickly pulled her hand back. Riley looked down at her skin – no mark was visible. Hesitantly, she tried once again to touch the handle. No heat. Confused, she tapped the handle several more times before she entered the church. Inside was a tall, older man, dressed in black clerical clothing. Riley found him behind the altar, bowing before a cross and blessing himself repeatedly. She approached him nervously and greeted him.

"Miss Orel?" he repeated after her introduction, "the girl from this morning," he added.

Riley shrugged uncomfortably.

The man gave her an odd look. "Should start then," he said. His tone seemed to have changed; it was stern.

She nodded innocently, and he led her to the confessional by the front entrance of the church. The man entered one side, leaving Riley to enter on her own. She went around to the second door, touched the handle, and sighed in relief; she had expected it to be hot. She touched the wooden door. It felt warm and somehow uncomfortable to her. She began to feel prickles against the tips of her fingers. The tingling intensified until it began to sting. She pulled away quickly. The man called her name, and as he did so, Riley could have sworn she heard a voice shouting "No!" from somewhere beyond the church's walls. She slowly raised her hand to touch the handle once again. It now felt quite cold. She pressed the door open and entered the dark booth. She could see the man's silhouette through a small screen window on the wall separating them. The door shut, and Riley began thinking of what to say.

"It's been at least a month now," she paused, "I had a nightmare. Well first it wasn't that scary. I was running through a forest trying to get away from a monster. It looks like someone covered with a black cloak, just like the grim reaper, but it has bird feet. When I woke up, I didn't think anything of it. The next day, I dreamt I saw a man in an alley, but I couldn't see any of his features. The only thing I could make out was his clothes. His face and body were just a blur," she explained nervously. After a few deep breaths she continued. "That very same creature I saw in the dream from the night before came after him. Whatever it is, it had no use for those green, birdlike feet that dangled at the bottom of its cloak because it just hovered a foot off the ground. Yesterday, I saw him in the newspaper – the man I mean – not that cloaked ghost. Anyway, the man, he died in an alley," she said breathlessly.

She looked at the priest's silhouette and tried to read the impression of his face. He did not seem to care much. He was completely still and was staring at what seemed to be a picture frame hanging in front of him. Although the priest did not seem to be paying much attention, she felt relieved. She sat silent for a moment then raised her head to face the wall once again. "I had another dream like that. It was horrible. I heard screams. The faces were just blurs, yet I could tell them apart from each other, and somehow, I could see their facial expressions," she explained.

"Listen to me," he interrupted. "You say that you can't see what they look like. But Miss Orel, if you can't see their faces, then how is it that you know the man in yesterday's newspaper is the man killed by the 'ghost,' as you call it?"

"I don't know, sir. I have asked myself the same thing," Riley answered.

"How many of these dreams have there been, then?" he asked, suddenly showing interest in her problem.

"I've had a few, but only this one actually came true. I had another dream where I was in some dark place. It was terrifying – not during the dream though. I hadn't noticed how scared I was 'till I woke up. In this dream, there was a blue portal-shaped light in front of me." She stopped as she saw the man look her way.

"Go on," he insisted.

"Well something... um... a hand reached out of it and many whispering voices called my name all at once."

"I see." He looked at his watch. Riley felt crazy. She shut her eyes for a moment and told him about the dream where the fly had changed into a ghost once it got close enough to her. Unexpectedly, the priest got up. "I have another appointment in three minutes. Why don't you come back at noon tomorrow?" he added urgently. He exited the booth without giving Riley a chance to confirm.

Coming here was a bad idea. She felt stupid, and the priest did not seem to care. Riley walked out and around the booth and turned the corner toward the entrance doors. Her nostrils were flaring, her face was beet red, and she unexpectedly bumped into someone on her way. It was a gorgeous young woman with fiery red hair. She embodied the term redhead, and her appearance was strikingly beautiful. The woman's complexion was slightly darker than Riley's, and she donned a large smile as they apologized to each other. Riley stared back into the young woman's light, hazelnut eyes. She looked familiar, yet Riley knew that she had never seen the woman before; a bubbly person with features like that stands out in a small town. Riley watched the redhead walk toward the priest, turned away, and made her way to the church parking lot. Her emotions overpowered whatever curiosity she had for that red hair on the young woman's head.

She opened her car door. A mixture of fury and embarrassment kept pulsing through her, and she could faintly hear people screaming in her mind. Very slowly, the face of the stranger in the church began to form across that of a screaming character from her nightmares. A man's voice suddenly shouted her name, breaking the image. She turned to see who was calling her and saw someone running toward her from the church doors.

In shock, Riley grabbed her forehead tightly with her left hand as whispers began to flow from everywhere. Her eyes darted from left to right, trying to focus on one voice at a time. She lowered her hand that now rested on her mouth. It was as if she was reliving her nightmare of the two lovers. She found herself standing in the middle of a forest. It was dark, and the air was cooler than usual. All was quiet as she climbed a hill. A woman's scream echoed from the top of the largest hill. Riley raced toward the shriek and now recognized that its source was the same woman she had just bumped into at the church. The woman was running down the hill with Riley's stepbrother, Craig. Riley ran closer to the hill and saw the demon appear from the bushes at the top of the slope. The creature descended faster than Craig and the woman could run. Riley sped up toward them. Unaware of Riley's presence, the ghost jabbed its sharp hand into Craig's back as he pushed the redheaded woman away from him. Riley caught up to the scene and tried to push the demon away. She fell through it and landed on the cold wet ground. Riley got up again and tried to grab Craig, but her hands could not even touch him. She yelled at the woman for help, but the woman could not hear Riley through the sound of her own screaming and crying. Craig turned pale, and the demon began to hover above him. It lifted Craig up then threw him back to the ground while pointing to the redhead. In its bone shivering voice, it said it was coming for her. Riley tried tending to her stepbrother, but she could not touch him. With tears in her eyes, she turned and saw the demon making its way toward the woman. It threw its hands in front of its cloak-covered face and drew a high scream.

"Riley!" called out a deep voice.

She blinked and realized she was still in the church parking lot. She looked around and felt someone's hand on her shoulder. She looked over and saw Craig, who seemed confused. Riley's eyes widened. She grabbed her stepbrother and hugged him tight.

"Craig! Oh, god I thought it killed you!" she cried out as a tear slid down her cheek.

Craig hugged her back and asked, "What are you talking about?"

Riley let go of him and wiped her cheek. She was at a loss. She could not explain what was happening to her.

"Uh..." she hesitated. "I had a nightmare so vivid that I thought you were dead this morning. Didn't I call you up to tell you about it?" she asked, trying to make light of the subject.

"No," he said, chuckling. "I haven't spoken to you in a while now. Did Liz give you the invite?"

"Yeah, she came over yesterday morning. Congratulations, by the way. Is that woman in the church Parker?"

"Thanks, and if you mean the redhead, yeah, that's Parker. I've been seeing her for about ten months now."

"Ten! Are you serious? Craig, I've never met her. My god, yeah it's been a while," she exclaimed.

"Well, we'll have to make plans sometime soon," he smiled. "I've got to go. We're going to meet with Monsignor to see how everything's going down for the big day," he explained happily, as he started at the church.

Riley said goodbye and got into her car. She rested her head on the back of the seat. Questions flooded her mind. *Is it a warning? What is happening to me? Am I going crazy?*

Chapter 3

◊ ◊ ◊

Riley sped down the dirt trail off Wrigley Lane in an attempt to clear her head from all the nonsense. She increased her speed as a rush of adrenaline came over her. The air was humid, and the ground was dusty. She felt the wind in her face through the opened window. Riley felt like she had leaped backward in time. *Faster. Faster*! She wished she could feel this way forever.

As she neared the city limit, she swerved recklessly to avoid colliding with a person, who seemingly appeared from nowhere. Dust clouded her view. In a panic, she quickly got out of the car and looked around. Nothing. She dropped to her knees to check underneath her car. *Thank god*. She pinched the bridge of her pointed nose and wiped her eyes in relief that she had not killed anyone. Her relief quickly turned to discomfort as shivers began to crawl up and down the back of her head. Riley warily looked over her right shoulder and gasped; a dozen feet behind her car stood a man looking in her direction. Thankful that she had not hit him with her car, Riley immediately began to run toward the person. She stopped, however, when she noticed the figure's features. The thing before her was manlike. He wore a black trench coat and a flat-rimmed gaucho hat. Riley was most disturbed by his paleness and lack of facial features.

"What do you want?" she screamed at the top of her lungs.

"Go back," the faceless creature commanded in a deep voice. It then turned around and walked toward Fallsdale.

Riley breathed deeply as she watched the man-shaped creature slowly fade into the distance. She pushed her bangs out of her face, turned back toward her car, and walked quickly with determination.

Riley drove cautiously back up the dirt road while keeping an eye out for the faceless hat-man. She reached the intersection on Wrigley Lane, where she tried convincing herself that what she had just seen was not real.

All of a sudden, she heard a honking sound from a car. She looked in her rear-view mirror and gasped at the sight of the faceless hat-man sitting in a small black car, parked behind her. He was gesturing for her to move her car forward. Feeling a burst of courage, she immediately got out of the car and approached the faceless man.

"What do you want me to do? Leave me alone!" she screamed.

The man, who now appeared to be just a regular human, rolled down the window. "I need to get home. Now move your god damn car!" he shouted back, spit flying out of his mouth.

"Oh god, I'm so sorry sir. I thought you were someone else," she said embarrassingly. Quickly, she turned and walked to her car as the man rolled up his window while muttering to himself.

No sooner had Riley gotten out of the fat, greasy man's way by right turning onto Wrigley, did she see what seemed to be the hat-man once again driving the car behind her. She stared wide-eyed as the horrid being turned left toward Georgia. She stopped. Riley turned her head and saw the faceless being now standing by the Fallsdale limit sign. His car, however, continued to travel toward Georgia. She looked at the clock in her car and saw that it was getting late: 6:36 p.m. She was inexplicably tempted to see what the hat-man wanted. As she turned the vehicle around, he began walking toward Georgia.

Riley followed the hat-man but it seemed as though no matter how fast she drove, she would never reach him. The man was always a certain distance from her, and even in the dark of the night he was as visible as day. Riley felt uneasy. Coming up to a stop, where the hat-man had begun crossing the little wooden bridge of Georgia park, Riley sat petrified. *What possessed me to follow him?* She parked next to the bridge and stepped out of her car. She watched him stand motionless at the end of the bridge, staring up at the moon. She peered up and looked at the starry sky. Riley gazed at the beautifully lit sky with fascination; this was not a view you normally saw in cloudy, boring Fallsdale. The man began to walk forward. She crossed the bridge and walked onto the rocky path. The hills and forest surrounding the park were very dark.

She remembered coming here when she was a child with her mother and father during the winter for bobsledding. She remembered the cold wind against her face and her father struggling to get her scaredy-cat mother to join him in a slide. She remembered the time she had used the slide that her father had forbidden her to ride on due to ramps at the bottom that the older children had built. She remembered finding herself shooting upwards and falling off the sled before it had landed. As she lost herself in childhood memories, a voice suddenly shook her back to reality. "Come!" she heard the hat-man say in a higher voice. He sounded much closer than he was. She could not help but obey the man. She came up to the first small slope and stood beside him at the top. He was abnormally still. Riley watched him staring at the sky. She should have felt frightened, yet there was only peace inside of her. She was within inches of the scariest being she had ever encountered, but something about this strange creature attracted her. She looked up to the stars and back to the man, who was now staring at her. He turned away as she returned his gaze.

"Why have you brought me here?" she asked.

While keeping his position, he answered, "I'm helping you." His voice sounded different again.

"How? Why here?" she questioned as she looked around.

"It's where you must be," he said, yet again in a new voice.

She looked at him. Today's events sprung immediately to mind. "Does this have to do with the nightmare?" The man turned his head toward her. "Are these dreams real?" she asked. "I mean, I'm not seeing the future, am I?"

He was completely visible in the moonlight, making Riley's stomach churn. Up until this moment, she never considered the validity of his being: was he just a figment of her imagination or actually something standing beside her? He looked so real. She began to feel nervous. Suddenly, in a blink of the eye, he went from looking at her to watching the sky. "Please," she pleaded, but even at this point, she was not sure what she was asking. Her voice began to tremble. He bowed his head and faded away. Riley was alone. She felt shivers on the back of her neck. She looked around for the hat-man, but he was gone. She backed away and stumbled down the hill with Craig continuously pulsing through her mind. The disgusting thought of him lying dead on the ground made her heart skip a beat. Just then, a blue light appeared in the sky. She looked up. Many bluish-white stars close to one another formed in a cluster. They reminded her of the light she had walked toward in her dream. All together, the stars began to dim until they were no longer there.

She bit her lower lip. *What if this actually happens?* She knew it sounded crazy to think that the cloaked creature in her dreams was real, but the man in the hat seemed extremely real just now. She traveled down the slope and crossed the bridge. Shivers continuously crawled down her spine, but the sooner she got to her car, the sooner she would be safe. She hopped in, shut the door, and grabbed the cell phone on the dashboard. She immediately found Craig's number in her contact list and called him.

"Hello?" answered Craig.

"Craig! Ok listen, where are you?" she said anxiously.

"Just sitting around the house," he answered. "Why?"

"Um… are you going to Georgia anytime soon? With Parker? In the park? Maybe at night?" she asked hesitantly.

"Georgia Park? Yeah. We're going Tuesday. How'd you know?" he responded.

"Alright, I know this sounds weird but please don't go… not right now at least," she urged as she looked from left to right at the few cars that passed by.

"Alright Riles, what's going on?" he replied playfully, trying to dismiss Riley's apprehension.

"Seriously, I just have a really bad feeling. Please promise me you won't go," she pleaded.

"Riley," he said. "Listen, we'll talk later kay? Parker just called me upstairs for supper, and we're having guests. I got to go," he stammered.

The phone began to beep slowly. Riley pulled it away from her ear and looked at the screen. She exited to the main menu and placed it back on the dashboard.

Her mind felt numb. She was slightly red in the face and started to feel like she was overreacting. She turned the key, which she had forgotten in the ignition, but the car would not fire up. She turned the key several more times, but nothing happened. Suddenly, the familiar shivers began crawling up and down her spine. After minutes of fighting with the ignition, the engine rumbled. A great pressure lifted from her. She pushed her hair back and began to back out of the lot. Riley tried to ignore the shivers, but as she turned the car around, a horrible image caught her attention. The image of floating eyes in the darkness clouded her rear-view mirror. She froze, and her jaw dropped an inch. Her heart skipped a beat, and her thoughts went blank. She grabbed the gear shift and slowly put the car back into reverse.

Riley pressed the accelerator. The car lurched backward. A satisfying thud sounded from the rear bumper, and the entire backend shot into the air as the back tires passed over the carcass of whatever was out there. The front tires promptly followed suit. *That should take care of the monster.*

Riley stopped the car. She leaned forward, trying to see the body from her driver's seat. No such luck. *Damn.* She would have to get out. *Get out*, she chided herself. *Am I this stupid?* Riley chewed her lower lip. If she did not get out, she would never know what the creature was. *It's not worth it.* She decided to sit and wait for the creature to become visible in her headlights.

Riley pressed the accelerator again, and an even louder thump issued from her rear bumper. The jarring impact caused her to fling forward until her seatbelt yanked her to a stop. She whipped her head around. A tree loomed over her car, completely dominating the view from her rear window. Its knotted trunk seemed to leer at her with a mocking face. This was not happening. Her insurance rates were already sky high. She could not afford another claim.

Riley swore loudly and then remembered why she was there in the first place: the dead monster. She glanced out the front windshield, but the monster was still not visible.

"This is stupid, Riles," she told herself aloud. She was terrified, but something inside of her would not allow her to leave without the knowledge of what was out there. She sucked in her breath, pulled the door handle, and opened the door. It opened all of three inches before it collided with another tree. "Damn!" It was dark, and there were trees everywhere. She crawled over the seats and out the passenger door to free herself from the car.

She stopped momentarily to survey the damage to the trunk.

She knew it was a waste of time in the dark, and she was afraid to see what she had hit. *What if it's not even there anymore? What if it's angry? Get a grip, Riley. The sooner you look at this thing, the sooner you can get out of here.*

Riley edged around to the front of the car. There, bathed in the twin headlights of her car, was a raccoon. There was no monster. She had killed an ordinary raccoon. A flood of relief mixed with guilt washed over her. "Just a goddamn raccoon!" She let out a chuckle, turned, and headed back for the car.

As she began to crawl back in through the backseat, a disturbing question crept into her mind. *How had an ordinary raccoon lifted the entire backend of my car off the ground*? She covered her gaping mouth with her hand and hurried back into the driver's seat. Riley quickly put the vehicle into gear and drove off.

The moon lit up the road with a bluish glow. Riley drove toward Fallsdale, hoping to get home as soon as possible. The images she had just seen were burning in her mind. The man without the face frightened her. She wondered why she had followed him when she could have gone straight home. At the time, she had been more curious than afraid. The closer she had gotten to him, the less she had worried about potential danger. She wondered about the significance of the park and desired nothing more than to get back home.

As she pulled up into Fallsdale, the clock on Gordon's Bank on Wrigley Lane struck eight o'clock. She admired the full moon in the sky as she drove down the old street. Beautiful antique street lamps lit up the road. This area of town was Riley's favourite place to go out for lunch or coffee. Every now and then, she would come here to take photos. As she gazed into a clothing shop that she slowly passed, her phone began to vibrate. She grabbed it anxiously, expecting Craig to be on the other end, but instead, she found a message from her mother: *Hey bud. I don't like watching you and Tim fight. Could we get together some time?*

Riley took her eyes off the message and focused on to the road as she turned onto the next street. She soon began messaging back: *Ever since I've left home, things have been great so... sorry, not now.* She sent the message and immediately turned off the phone. Giving her mother attitude about seeing her step father again pained Riley. She knew well that six years was long enough for anyone to change, but something kept her from liking Tim.

Riley pulled up in front of her house as she shoved the cell into her pants pocket. She parked the car, got out onto the grass, and opened the front door. The house was quiet and dark. She quickly flicked on the hallway lights which brightened the living room enough for her to turn on the lamp by her dark blue couch. Being alone did not feel as terrifying with the lights on. She sat on the couch while shivers crawled up and down her back. Riley scanned the room, but no one was around. The open drapes made her feel vulnerable. She got up and covered the window with the brown curtains and rushed back to her couch. She sat silently for a moment as she calmed down. Riley lay down on the sofa, covered herself with the blanket, and tried to get some sleep despite the discomforting feeling she had of being watched. She rolled over onto her back and opened her eyes. Her jaw dropped. There was a little black fly on ceiling directly over her. She slowly sat up while staring at the little monster. Enraged, she got off the couch and walked into the main hallway, all the while watching the fly on the ceiling. She grabbed one of her dirty sneakers from the shoe rack and returned to the living room. She stood underneath the fly for a few moments and then threw the shoe up at the little devil. The shoe missed, bounced off the ceiling, and landed on the wooden floor. "Where are you all coming from?" she yelled. The fly buzzed around then flew out of the room into the hall before it rested itself on the front door. She walked over and tried to smack it, but the fly was too quick. Into the kitchen, she chased the fly, and turned on the lights. She looked around and found it leading her into the hallway, toward the bathroom and bedroom. Riley stopped; that hallway had no light switch. She suddenly felt shivers throughout her body once again. Slowly, she backed away from the dark hall and headed back to the safety of her comfortable couch in the living room.

Morning broke, and Riley rose from the couch, opened the curtains, and immediately went into the kitchen to turn off the lights that were no longer needed. She opened the fridge, pulled out the last of her plates of cinnamon buns, and placed it on the countertop. She removed the plastic wrap and placed two of the buns in the microwave. From the wooden cupboard above the microwave, she glumly grabbed a coffee mug and ground coffee beans. Reaching into an identical set of cupboards beneath the countertop, Riley pulled out a coffee filter and made her drink in the small space next to the warming cinnamon buns. The microwave beeped three times, indicating that her breakfast was ready. She ate at her kitchen table while looking sadly at the happily married couple on yesterday's paper.

Not even her favourite warm breakfast could keep the rush of chills subdued any longer. She turned to look toward the dimly lit hallway and wiped the coffee off of her mouth using her sleeve. After a short breather, she stood from her chair and peered into the hall. *Doesn't seem too dark.* It was not the dim light that made her feel uncertain – it was the closed doors which most likely led into dark rooms behind them. She walked slowly toward the first door on the left. She touched the handle, turned it very gently, and abruptly pulled it open. Inside were cleaning supplies and canned food on shelves. She shut the door. Her panting breath had calmed down, and she regained enough courage to continue down the small hallway. She went to the next door to her right and swung it open. The room was dark, and she cowered away from the doorway. She leaned against the wall next to the opened door and suddenly felt her mind settle back into her body. *What am I doing?* She pushed herself off the wall, went into the dark room, and turned on the light. She drew the shower curtain on the right-hand side across from the white porcelain toilet. Nothing was around – not even a fly. She made her way to the last door on the left and entered the room. The light crept in though the edges of the brown curtains, making the room visible enough to avoid the piles of clothes on the ground. She walked by her bed, circled a small pile of white clothes, and pulled the drapes to one side of the window. Riley looked around and smirked.

As she pulled out a clean shirt from her dresser and searched for a pair of dark blue jeans beneath her bed, a sudden rush of cold air raced against her body for a split second. At that very moment, her attention was directed to the top of her dresser, where the little black fly lay upside down. Wide mouthed, she walked over to examine it. She could not believe her eyes. She picked it up, rushed over to the garbage can in the kitchen, and threw the little sucker out. *That better be the last of them.*

Happy to have a fly-less house for the time being, she stood in front of her bedroom mirror with a large smirk across her face. She examined her outfit and was pleased with her jeans and white knit shirt. She spun around in front of the mirror and pulled her bangs back behind her ear, but they fell back out of place. As she struggled with her bangs, she noticed movement behind her reflection. Worried, she spun around but saw nothing. She returned to face the mirror and again saw something rush through her doorway and into the hall. She quickly stuck her head through the doorway but saw nothing. On edge, she made her way to the kitchen and grabbed her cold coffee. She sipped the last of it and sat the mug down in the sink. Deciding to continue her daily routine as though she had seen nothing, Riley picked up her dirty plate and added it to the sink, put a new filter and some coffee grinds in her machine, and wiped up the counter top. Familiar shivers began to crawl up and down the back of her head. She turned around quickly; nothing was there.

Riley reflected on something her father told her as a child: *When faced with something that frightens you, hum or whistle a tune and everything will be alright.* Making it up as she went along, Riley shut her eyes and began to hum. She spun in circles and moved around happily as the tune carried her back to a time when her father was still alive. Warmth rushed over her. She could imagine her father standing in her own kitchen and smiling back at her. She opened her eyes, feeling an enormous pressure in her throat. She felt like crying. She held her tune and felt somewhat happy when remembering her childhood. A tapping noise coming from behind interrupted her nostalgia. She looked around, but the buzzing sound of the refrigerator was all that made noise. As she began to hum once more, the tapping sound resumed. She continued humming as she washed her coffee cup and plate in the sink, embracing the mysterious tapping as though it was setting the beat to her melody. Continuing to hum, she turned off the faucet and quickly turned around. A thick, brown human-like form retreated backward and into the main hallway. The smoke-like creature made no sound. She was frightened yet shocked that it had run from her. *Was it trying to hurt me?* In spite of the potential danger and the quick beating of her heart, Riley was tempted to follow it in order to find out what it might have been.

Riley walked over to the living room doorway and took a few deep breaths before entering. The thing was not around, but a delayed fear finally fell on her and she rushed out the front door. *What happened there? What would posses me to follow that thing so willingly?* She jumped into her car and struggled to turn it on. "Come on, come on," she whispered to herself. The car started. She was relieved to find that noon was nearing. Almost certain this was not her imagination, Monsignor should hear about it.

Just a month or so ago, she had not a care in the world – at least none involving a demon striking her as she slept. She loved her job; photography was her favourite thing in the world. She had become an expert on the computer as well and could fix up photos to look all the more perfect. She had been content. Now, she felt insane. Riley wondered if she was being punished by a higher power. *But for what? Did I anger some powerful being with my lack of faith?* She pulled up into the church parking lot and stared at the building. For reasons beyond her comprehension, this place now felt safe to her. Despite her lack of religious values, she was drawn to the church she had always believed was corrupted. Riley got out of the car and walked over to the front entrance. She reached for the handle and was relieved to find that it was cool. Out of the corner of her eye, she thought she saw something scurry around the corner of the church. She quickly pushed the doors open and entered the old building.

Riley walked down the aisle and gazed at the stained glass along the walls. The priest was not around. She sat in the first pew and waited. Only a moment had passed when the priest entered the sanctuary from the back. He walked with power in his stride as he neared her. He breathed deeply, and in a rude tone, he told her to approach him. Dumbfounded, Riley rose from the seat and walked over to the old man. He took a brief moment to stare at her with what appeared to be wonder and worry in his eyes, and then he demanded to hear about the dreams once more. Riley looked at him and asked, "Am I going crazy?" The man stared down at her, and in the same angry tone, he commanded her to do as he said. Riley hesitated. She took a deep breath and began explaining her first nightmare. He rubbed the top of his forehead as she described the creature, then he cut her off with a wave of his hand. Nervously, Riley looked over to the cross on the altar and could have sworn she caught a glimpse of the brown figure run away from behind it. A hateful concentration formed across her face. She was about to burst into a rant about the brown smoke figure when the priest noticed the strain on her face. The priest's demeanour became much more serious, and he ordered her to look at him while he spoke.

"These shadow creatures – are they all you've seen?" he asked.

She hesitated. "No. There was a smoky brown one. I swear, I'm not making this up," she pleaded. "Then there's the hat-man."

The man looked at her curiously and insisted that she explain. She first spoke about the brown figure that terrified her and then began to talk about the faceless man that brought her to Georgia. She explained how her fear had only developed after the faceless man had left and that neither one of these creatures had come to her in dreams. The man's eyes widened. "Sir, I don't know what to think anymore," she said.

The man looked at her tenderly. "It's ok," he said in a soft voice. "You're just delusional. You are crazy, but don't worry, you have no idea how many people like you come to the church for help, Miss Orel. I will be seeing you again. Good friends of mine will explain why these sorts of things are happening to you." Riley did not know how to react to this. She was reassured, knowing that the visions were not real, and above all, she felt happy that her family would be safe. Craig would live past his thirties with his fiancé. Yet there was something about being called crazy that was not satisfying one bit. She thanked the priest and left him her home phone number so he could contact her for their next meeting. The man smiled, and she walked away.

A goal seemed to have been fulfilled, and the weight on her shoulders disappeared. For reasons beyond her understanding, Riley actually felt content.

Chapter 4

Riley drove carefully down Evermount Street, while talking to Craig's voicemail. "I'm sorry for last night, just forget about it. I'll explain some other time. Anyhow see you later." She ended the call and set the phone down in the cup holder, when suddenly, in the middle of the road, the faceless man appeared. He shook his head at her. She stopped the car and stared at the man that stood a dozen feet ahead. "You're not real," she hissed. He vanished. A slow, drive-by inspection of the area where he had been standing revealed nothing out of the ordinary.

After a few moments of driving, Riley arrived at home. She entered her house and immediately shut the door. Her mind relaxed as she stared out at the autumn scenery from the kitchen window. Her sweet smile was cut short by a familiar tapping noise, which seemed to be coming from one of the front rooms. As she walked into the hallway, the tapping sound amplified. She slowly crept toward the living room entrance and peered in. The sound stopped. Standing by the doorway, Riley scanned the room, but she could not find the source of the tapping. *The priest said this is all in my mind. This isn't real.* After reassuring herself, she entered the room. She looked around but found nothing suspicious. As she turned around, the tapping sound started up again. Her instincts quickly spun her to face the window, and she saw it – a little black fly on the outside, repeatedly lunging itself toward the glass.

Riley could not believe there were other people going through the same thing that she was. It all seemed too intense and too real to just be some strange mental condition. She watched the fly flinging itself at the window. It began to slow down and rested on the window sill. "Stupid thing knocked itself out," she said to herself. As she sat on the couch and watched television, her imagination began to wander, and her eyelids got heavy. Her eyes closed every few moments. She lay down on the sofa and watched the television blur until she fell asleep.

Once again, she was in a dark place; nothing could be seen except for herself. She saw her white, knit shirtsleeves, her jeans, and her hands. A mirror appeared next to her which reflected the image of her face. She touched her pointy nose and brushed her bangs behind her right ear. She looked behind herself and saw nothing but darkness. Terror filled her body as she glanced back at the mirror and saw not her own face, but the head of the faceless man staring back at her. Covering her mouth to stop herself from screaming, Riley forced herself to calm down. She pulled her arms to her sides and looked back into the mirror, but the man was no longer there – he now stood in physical form right beside her. As he shook his head, the voice of a little girl screamed, "NO!" The voice echoed from every direction before coming to a sudden stop.

From out of the darkness, many voices burst into a chaotic conversation. "Did you hear that darling?" asked a young woman's voice.

"Mommy, I'm scared!"

"It's ok, everything will be fine," replied a mother to a young boy.

Hundreds of men, woman and children spoke at once with their voices overlapping. The man stood still and watched Riley. She looked around but knew there was not anyone else with her. She was alone with the faceless man. Within the screams, Riley could hear distinct voices of men and women calling out after each other, seemingly finishing each other's sentences. "Can you please…" said the voice of a woman.

"Go away!" shouted an older man.

"Help her!" cried a teenage girl.

"Can't stop now!" from the voice of a young boy.

"Time is running out," said a man's voice.

"You'll regret it, you know," said a young woman.

Riley stared at the pale creature frightfully. "What the hell are you?" she hissed. The man vanished.

The surrounding darkness was slowly pushed out of the area by a bright light which focused into her living room. The curtains were wide open, and the sun brightened the room. Riley found herself lying down on the sofa. The commercials on the television made very little sound. A faint beeping was coming from somewhere nearby. She sat up, opened the coffee table, and found her old digital watch. It was ringing its morning alarm that had not been set for the longest of time. The date flashing on the screen said it was Tuesday. She wondered if the watch was correct – had she slept away an entire day? A blurry figure ran out of the living room and into the hallway. She turned off the television set and walked into the kitchen, attempting to follow whatever she had seen. Deep down, she hoped to find the shadow that she kept seeing. Nothing was around. The home phone indicated the same date as the old watch: Tuesday August 24. Riley let her imagination wander off. She envisioned the faceless man and the brown, clouded figure. They were both very mysterious, yet they were also very different from one another. The thick shadow would stare at her from behind a corner, whereas the hat-man would reveal his presence and sometimes speak. Riley wondered what she had done to end up with these disturbing visitors.

The day went by very slowly. She caught sight of something running away from her a few times. These sightings brought on thoughts of the priest. Riley wondered if he could help her and hoped that he was right. She sat at the table for lunch, waiting to see if the brown shadowy figure would appear again. She went through her daily routine, washed a few dishes, and swept up a little. Eventually, as she crouched in the hallway sweeping up dust into the dust bin, she felt the back of her head go numb. Through the corner of her eye, she could see something unusual. Her whole body shivered. *What if all these strange apparitions are just my subconscious warning me that I've forgotten something important? Maybe if I speak to it, it will tell me something I need to know.* Without turning toward the thick shadow, she asked, "Can I see you?" There was no response, but she did notice it moving around behind her. "I won't hurt you," she explained. She slowly turned toward it as she stood up on her feet. The strange creature peered innocently at her from beside the living room doorway. It was incredible. The being had very sharp looking ears, and it stood at Riley's height. Its body had a smoky consistency, and it came forward curiously like a child. They examined each other from a distance. It was manlike, completely naked, and it had a smoky composition and missing facial features, just like the hatman. Riley was speechless. They stood staring at each other for a few moments. He examined the hallway and looked back at her. He seemed to contemplate something. He lifted an uncertain, smoky finger to the front door. She looked back at him, but he was gone.

The sun was setting, and Riley could not get the horrible picture of her stepbrother dying out of her mind. If she stayed home and the priest was wrong, she would go crazy. She would not be able to live while knowing that something could have been done to save him.

She looked at the white door at the end of the hall and stood up from her kitchen chair. She was going to Georgia Park, although certain nothing would happen. She walked over to the closet in the main hallway and pulled out her light brown leather jacket. She quickly walked out the door, jumped into her car, and drove off.

Worries flowed through Riley's mind. She sped down Evermount Street, Diligent Road, and Brookfield Road until she reached Wrigley Lane, which brought her straight to Georgia Park. The sun was fading away. Although she believed the priest, she had to see for herself. She came to a complete stop next to the little wooden bridge and got out of her car. Just like in her dream, the air was very cool. The sun was barely on the horizon. As she was about to cross the bridge, she noticed a red pickup truck just like Craig's a short distance down the road. She walked over to the vehicle and sure enough, it was Craig's truck.

Next to the truck was a little bike trail in the bushes which Craig and Parker must have gone through. A strong feeling of déjà vu came upon her. She walked onto the path, feeling very strange as she stepped over the thorn branches and followed the trail up a small slope. After a while, she came to an opening that seemed very familiar. As she looked at the hills, her memory began to experience a strange replay of her nightmare at the church, showing her every detail she had previously missed.

She ran forward to the place where she would soon hear the redheaded woman's scream. Riley had never actually been up this way before, yet she knew just where to go. She slowly walked, listening for any noise, but everything was completely silent. A few bats flew overhead, and some squirrels chased each other in and out of the bushes. Once she got to the top of the first small hill, the large hill with the bush of trees at the top became visible. She began to panic. Her breathing quickened. She walked down the slope with her eyes peeled on the large hill. It was a short distance away, but no screams of terror were heard.

Riley hoped this was a waste of time. It was mysterious that she knew the layout of the park, but there did not seem to be any ghosts chasing after anyone or screams echoing through the air. Her nerves, however, were still on edge. As she stopped to take a few deep breaths, it all happened at once. A large tree branch broke overhead, causing Riley to look up at the hill in terror. She heard a loud, piercing, and familiar scream. Her bones trembled – it was the redhead. Out of the bushes came two people running for their lives down the hill toward Riley. Her jaw dropped as she heard a dark voice from the top of the hill hissing with rage. Instantly, the dark demon from her dreams appeared from out of the cluster of trees and raced down toward Craig and Parker. Riley's heart sunk. *No*. It was real, but it seemed so impossible.

She ran upwards, not even hesitating when the creature gained speed. "Craig, move! Hurry, out of the way!" Riley screamed at the top of her lungs, but it was too late. The ghost had begun lifting Craig off the ground as Riley reached them. Just like in the dream, she hurdled herself at the creature but fell through onto the ground. She jumped back up and grabbed onto Craig's arms to try pulling him down, but the demon raised him higher before throwing him down on top of her. Riley began to cry as she touched his pale face. "I should have stopped you from coming!" she cried. Craig was dead. She watched the cloaked creature hovering toward Parker with its birdlike feet clenched beneath its robes. It was then that Riley noticed him – at the bottom of the hill, the hat-man was staring upwards. She stared back at him with tears in her eyes. She looked back at Craig, wiped his cold, sweaty face, and looked back down to the faceless man, who moved several feet closer in a blink of the eye. The demon stopped moving as the hat-man became noticeable to Parker, who was crying on the wet ground. The demon backed away for a moment as the hat-man pointed his crooked finger at it. The hat-man looked from Riley to Parker and nodded. He looked back at the demon, straightened his arms to his sides, and shot himself right into the demon's core, causing it to shriek a painful, deafening sound that made Riley cover her ears. She shut her eyes to try blocking out the image she caught of the creature screaming and running back up the hill into the forest. She noticed why the demon never seemed to use its feet. From what she saw, on its talons, the demon ran awkwardly and kept stumbling.

Riley touched Craig's face with her shaky hands and saw the redheaded woman crawling painfully up to them. Tears slid across both the women's faces. Riley cried into her hands as Parker held on tightly to Craig. Riley wiped her tears and saw Parker pulling out her phone from her pocket. She seemed to be in so much pain. Her voice shook and cracked as she spoke. After a dozen minutes, they were out of there. Riley knew now that this was certainly real: the hat-man, the demon, the shadow back at home, and her dreams. Craig was dead. It was all real.

Riley sat in the waiting area in the Fredsfurd Hospital, waiting for Parker. She sat alone in the corner, looking out the bay window. The news on the television showed another mysterious death of a 25-year-old Caucasian man down on Frank Boulevard. Riley was both saddened but amazed that she had not foreseen that man's death. Maybe it was over. Perhaps she had to believe in the dream to become free of the curse. *But what if he wasn't even murdered by a demon?* She could not think straight. Craig was really gone, and she did not know what to expect anymore. A younger looking man with short, light blonde hair and pale blue eyes approached Riley and concernedly asked, "Are you Parker white's friend? My name's Marc Braxton, I'm her doctor."

Riley stood up. "Can I see her?" she asked.

The doctor shook his head. "No, she's sleeping."

Riley felt like she was going crazy. She really needed someone to confirm what she saw. Only Parker could do that. "Are you sure? I'll only be a moment."

"I'm sorry, but I can't allow it." The doctor looked thoughtful for a moment. "You were with her when she got hurt, right?"

Riley nodded, but she didn't like where this was going.

"It might help if I knew exactly what happened to her."

"She was mauled," Riley said. "By an animal," she added, almost too quickly. What else would she be mauled by? A ghost? She might as well ask where the psycho ward was now and save some time.

The doctor furrowed his brow. He appeared dubious. "What type of animal?"

"A...A..." *A what? Bear, lion.* "A dog. A big one. I think it was a rot."

"Never seen a dog make a wound like that."

Riley shrugged. The doctor stared at her.

Go ahead and stare. She was through answering his questions. "Can I please see her?"

"We'll let you know when she can have visitors." He turned and walked away.

Riley sat alone in the waiting area for two hours after that. The large open doorway to her right, led to a room filled with desks behind a thick sheet of glass where all the secretaries worked. Riley left the waiting room to take a little walk around the hospital. The clock at the end of the first hallway indicated 2:00 a.m. Time swung by very slowly in these cold, lonely halls. She ended up walking in a complete circle, ending up all the way back at the front entrance by the waiting area and the secretarial office. Many of the women who had been working behind the glass divider had already left, and someone had taped a list of committed patients to the window. At the very end of the list was Parker White, staying in room 26, section J on the second level. Riley looked up into the glass to see if anyone was around, but the few woman on the other side were busy working on computers. She looked back and verified the location before taking off through the doors.

Riley slowly passed the corridors on the second floor and ended up finding J without any problems. She walked down the hall and could see the number 26 on the very last door to her right. A very faint weeping was coming from inside the room. She pushed open the door and walked in.

The lights were off, and six nursing areas were hidden behind curtains. Creeks from bedsprings came from behind the curtains to the left of the room. Riley peeked through a gap between the two curtains which were pulled aside to hide the patient. Beautiful, fiery, red hair was tossed uncomfortably across the pillow on the other side. She slowly entered and saw Parker, who lay belly-down on a nursing bed. She tossed, turned, and moaned as she tried to touch her own back. Riley stood there for a moment, unknowing of what to do. Riley walked out of Parker's sleeping area to grab a cozy, burgundy chair by the entrance and set it next to Parker's bed. Parker painfully twisted to look over her shoulder to see who had entered her room. At the sight of Riley, she gasped and grabbed hold of her back with her hand. It was painful even for Riley to watch Parker struggle into a more comfortable position. Riley approached her slowly and gave a weak smile. Parker's eyes filled with tears.

"Is Craig alright?" she asked in a weak and crackling voice.

Riley had no idea what to say. She looked away from Parker for a short second and noticed that Parker understood what she was thinking. The redheaded woman struggled to hold back her tears, and she burst into quiet sobs. Riley sat down in a chair while covering her mouth. She too wanted to cry, but she just could not let herself even though the pressure in her throat was so intense. In an unnatural scene, Parker's body involuntarily lifted itself and her spine arched backward. Her stomach launched up a foot in the air, leaving her head and legs to give balance. Parker's screaming was terrifying, and she began to violently grip at her back. Riley panicked and jumped off her chair to grab hold of Parker. She struggled against the force of Parker's muscle spasms and was strong enough to flip Parker over onto her stomach. The spasms then stopped, and Parker lay shocked and silent on the bed. Her hospital bib separated and revealed her bare back which was covered with remnants of their horrible encounter. There were three large, blue, claw-shaped cuts with fiery edges slanted across her back from her top right shoulder to her left hip.

"Oh my god," said Riley as she examined the wounds.

Parker buried her head back into her pillow as she gasped at the pain. She turned her head onto its side and breathed deeply, trying to relax.

"Sorry, but I don't know who you are," she said weakly to Riley.

"I'm Craig's step sister, Riley." She said in a sad and shadowy voice. Riley sat back down in the burgundy chair next to Parker. "I'm so, so sorry," she said as she planted her face in her hands. She was still unable to cry. Parker lay silently as a few tears slid across her cheeks. Riley lifted her head with rage in her eyes and said "I could've stopped it, but I didn't – that damn old man!"

"No Riley," Parker said weakly. "I could've done something. I was petrified. I was too scared to move," she said in a shaky voice.

"But look at you, Parker. Look at where you are, you—"

"And look at where Craig is!" she interrupted.

"You couldn't have done anything more than me, trust me," she said in a tone of pure sorrow.

The room fell silent for a few moments. Parker stared at Riley with a weak and confused expression. Riley sighed and looked at her feet. As she moved her eyes back upward to meet Parker's gaze, an idea suddenly came to her. She sat up a little straighter and said, "listen, when we get you out of here, I need you to go somewhere with me." Parker stared at her with sleepy eyes and yawned.

"Ok, sure. Just, um..." She fell asleep before she could finish.

Chapter 5

Parker woke up to the sound of two people arguing with each other. Riley was no longer with her. She sat up slowly and felt a sharp pain in her back as she got out of bed, but aside from that, the rest of her body felt numb. She peaked out of the curtain-enclosed room and could see Riley speaking to a short, fat, peach-haired lady. Riley stared down at the woman with an evil glare. As the two women fought with each other, Parker walked over. They stopped immediately and stared at Parker.

"What's going on?" she asked, in a sleepy voice, while standing in the doorway.

"I fell asleep in the nursing room," Riley explained with a dramatic tone, mocking the fat woman.

"Miss, my colleague told you specifically not to wake her," the woman snapped.

"I didn't wake her up you little—"

"Okay, okay. Calm down," interrupted Parker. "She didn't wake me. I was already up. I barely slept at all last night," she said to the secretary.

After a short moment of silence, the nurse gave in. "You should get back to bed and I'll have Blondie here bring your breakfast," she said with a nod at Riley. Parker turned around while holding on to her aching back. The blue scratch marks showed trough the crack of her hospital bib.

Riley followed the fat nurse, who continuously gave her a hard time about her dirty clothes and knotted hair. Tuning out the nurse's criticisms, Riley wondered what had happened to the hat-man. She wondered if he had killed the beast. She followed the fat lady down the staircase to the main floor. They silently walked down a few hallways and came to two large shining silver doors that Riley had not noticed the night before. The fat lady walked into the room, and Riley followed. They were in the cafeteria; it was very clean and bright. The food smelled pretty good. The nurse told Riley to stay put as she left for the back room for a few minutes. Riley waited at one of the tables by the kitchen. The television set was hanging up on the wall across from her. It was set to the news channel. She sat and stared at the screen when suddenly, a breaking news report interrupted the regular broadcaster. The screen read: *Police say 25-year-old Jack Holton was found dead down on Frank Boulevard last night. Holton was murdered by Kevin O'Connor, a prisoner of Watson Way Prison.* Riley's heart began to pound. It couldn't be true; they must have made some mistake. *The cloaked demon had killed Holton – not just some man.* Deep down, she knew it was possible that a murderer had killed this man, but she felt sure that it had not been Kevin O'Connor but a demon out of her nightmares. She sat petrified, staring at the news. It worried her that she would have to go to sleep every night and watch someone new die at the sharp hands of a monster. The fat nurse came back into the room with a large blueberry muffin and a bowl of cereal on a tray. Riley slowly stood up while keeping her eyes on the television. She was handed the tray of food but kept directing her attention toward the news program. The fat lady gave a curious look at the television.

"O'Connor's some monster," she said in a surprisingly calm

and comfortable tone. "He's killed many people, and they continue to find his victims all over the place – the forest especially," she explained with a saddened voice.

Riley said nothing, but she gave the little, fat lady all of her attention. They stood silently for a few moments when the nurse looked at her watch – she had other patients to tend to. She handed Parker's food to Riley and left her to find the way back up to Parker's room.

Riley stared at the white and blue ceramic tiles on the floor as she made her way back up to Parker. The walls were ceramic and formed brilliant murals along the hallways; however, the doors leading to offices and nursing rooms were all a boring shade of beige. The stairs were carpeted a light grey all the way up to Parker's floor, and they led to two surprisingly bright red doors. Riley made her way through the hallways on the second floor, trying to find section J. She walked down the hallway straight to Parker's room and entered with the tray of food. After opening the curtain, she sat the tray down on the bedside table and sat herself down in the burgundy chair. Parker repositioned herself in the hospital bed and grabbed a piece of blueberry muffin. She looked curiously at Riley.

"Is everything alright?" she asked Riley, who blinked a few times before looking at her.

"I'm fine. I just thought that maybe it was all over," she said disappointingly.

"What was?" she asked through a mouthful of blueberry muffin. It was obvious that Parker was forcing herself to eat.

Riley stared at her for a moment with a quizzical expression. "I'm thinking of visiting Kevin O'Connor at the Watson Way Prison."

Parker looked at her vacantly. "Why would you go see him?" she asked as she sniffed the unappealing bowl of cereal.

"I need to know if he actually killed a man down on Frank Boulevard."

Parker shook her head. "But why?" She monotonously picked up the muffin and began to slowly eat more of it.

"I just want this madness to end. I need to talk to him."

"What? We were just attacked by some monster! Your brother was just killed! How can you be worried about some stranger who died out on the street?" Parker threw her hands up in front of her as though she would strangle Riley if she could get close enough. As memories of Craig flooded her mind, she fell back on the bed, defeated.

"I need for the man on Frank Boulevard to have been killed by the demon that we saw last night." She stood up. "If it killed him, then everything will be alright. I mean, even if the hat-man didn't kill it."

Parker looked puzzled and concerned. She looked at Riley, who seemed to be working something out in her mind, and she could not help but wonder if Riley was alright. Riley unexpectedly left the room, calling out, "I'll be right back" and swinging the curtains closed.

Parker said nothing. She listened to Riley's hurried footsteps until she could not hear them anymore.

Riley arrived at the hospital entrance when she remembered that she had been brought here by ambulance. She sighed and looked around in her pockets for some loose change. There was a lucky 50 cents in her jacket – just enough to make a call. She dialed the pay phone for a cab ride.

The taxi had Riley sitting in the waiting room for a half hour. She stared out the large window and waited impatiently. Her fingers tapped against the window sill as she watched the cars passing by. She sat, entirely displeased, when she heard a familiar voice ask, "You're still waiting around?" To her right, standing underneath the archway leading out of the waiting room, was Dr. Braxton.

"No," she replied. She was still a bit annoyed at the man. "My car isn't here. I'm waiting for a cab."

"Always fun. You see your friend this morning?" He tried to catch her eyes as she turned to look out the window.

Riley smirked slightly and turned around to see the smiling doctor. "Yes," she said.

With his hands in his pale green uniform pockets, he nodded awkwardly and said, "Yeah, um, she'll be coming out soon – just needs a little rest." Riley nodded back. "I'm sorry; I didn't get your name."

"Riley," she conceded after a small silence. "My cab's here," she said, pointing a thumb at the window behind her. "So, I'll just see you later then?"

"Yeah, see ya," he said, letting her pass.

She ran out to the cab and hopped in. A young Indian man sat in the driver's seat. He had long, greasy, curly, black hair that sprung from every angle as though he had not had a good night's rest all week. She could easily relate. His eyes were blood shot, and he did not even blink. He drove quickly, passing through many yellow lights at full speed on their way to the first stop at her place in Fallsdale. She looked back at the driver as she walked into her home and once again through the living room window. She tried to block his strange behaviour out of her mind and focus on the task at hand.

Riley lifted the base of the coffee table to search for her wallet. She brushed her hair back behind her ear and continued to look, but it wasn't there. A rush of anxiety came over her as she thought through all of the places she might have left it. In her bedroom, she tore through her dresser and night tables, but the wallet was nowhere to be found. She finally pulled out a dirty pair of jeans hiding underneath the bed and found it in one of the front pockets. Riley breathed a deep sigh of relief.

The sound of shattering glass coming from the kitchen made Riley jump from her knees to her feet. There was no sound of footsteps or voices, just silence followed the crash. She quickly snapped out of her petrified state and walked cautiously over to her doorway. She peered into the hall and could see a shadow against the wall. It was a person, and he or she was kneeling as if cleaning up the mess. Riley silently crept over to the end of the hallway to get a view of who was in her house. She breathed deeply a few times and jumped directly into a perfect view of the creature bent over the mess. Her eyes widened as the thick, smoke-like man stopped from trying to pick up the shards of glass and looked up to her with a tilted head. He backed away slowly on all fours and sprung out of sight once reaching the refrigerator behind him. In an instant, he had disappeared into the main hallway like a jaguar. Riley's breathing quivered as she stared at the kitchen doorway. She bent down to rest beside the pile of glass and began sweeping up the remains. One awfully sharp shard had settled on an angle and jabbed into her flesh as she swept over it with her hand. She gasped as she pulled the glass out of her skin.

Riley could see the thick brown shadow staring at her from the doorway. It was frightening, but she had adapted to it. She said nothing and threw all the shards she could gather into the garbage can. She slowly turned toward the door while feeling the lumpy wallet in her front pocket. She was thankful that when she looked up next, the creature was gone.

Back in the cab, the driver glared at her every few seconds through the rear-view mirror. As they left Fallsdale for Georgia Park, he began to twitch repeatedly. She was worried about seeing the park again, but she had to pick up her car. As the speed of the cab suddenly accelerated, the man stared into the rear-view mirror and smiled creepily. His great brown eyes stared deep into hers. His eyebrows rose. He steered the cab down the road while watching her sit uncomfortably in the corner of the back seat. There was a sudden shift in the air, and everything became even more uncomfortable. Riley began to feel lightheaded. For a minute, she forgot to breathe.

Everything felt still as the cab came to a stop on the side of the road. Her adrenaline raced; it was much too soon to be stopping now.

The driver bowed his head and opened the glove compartment. Riley watched him as he pulled himself back to look at her. He smiled and gazed into her piercing blue eyes as he raised a knife in his right hand. Riley stiffened in panic, and her jaw dropped. He began to reach for her face with the tip of the blade when she noticed the cloaked demon outside of the car. It was leaning in through the driver's window, making the same motions as the man only baring a sharp claw instead of a knife. Without hesitation, the driver lunged forward and shoved the blade toward her breast. She threw herself against the window just as the blade scrapped her leather jacket. Riley formed a fist with her hand and swung at the enemy. With a loud smack in the face, his head lay dangling over his shoulders. Even when knocked out, his body continued to mimic the motions of the demon outside. His arm swung the knife at her, and she continued to dodge his attacks while trying to escape the cab. The knife clipped her cheek and just missed her stomach by a few inches. Riley kicked the man's face upward and threw him back, giving her enough time to jump out of the cab.

She slammed the door closed as she saw him climbing over his seat to follow her. He reached the door, began pounding on the window, and screaming until he eventually tightened up and fell onto the car floor. She looked up to the demon that glided her way, its sharp birdlike feet clenched and dangling beneath its robes. It began to reach for her with its sharp, pale green hands. She tried backing away quickly but fell back onto the gravel next to the road. On the ground, she heard a rustling in the bushes nearby. The noise distracted the demon. It lifted its cloaked head and began to hover over to the source of the noise. Riley peered over to the rustling bushes as she began crawling away. It was the smoky brown figure hiding in the greenery. It hopped backward as it saw the demon coming for him. The smoke-like being hissed trough a mouthful of sharp teeth so large that it extended down his neck. The cloaked demon screeched loudly causing Riley to instinctively cover her ears. At the high pitched screech, the brown figure began to sprint away on all fours. It ran deep into the forest and out of sight. The demon paid no attention to Riley, who circled around the cab on her hands and knees. It slowly hovered over to the bushes and took off after the thick smoke-like creature, which had apparently saved her life.

Riley trembled with fear as she stared through the side windows of the cab. She was safe. Unexpectedly, the cab driver threw himself up at the window in front of Riley. She fell back onto the paved ground and hoped that he would not be able to get out. She stared petrified as he continued to smack his fists against the window until a small crack appeared in the centre of the glass. He looked at it curiously with his large brown eyes and began beating the window to enlarge the crack. She quickly crawled backward to the other side of the road. When she made it halfway across the road, Riley began to hear bits of glass hitting the pavement. The man had shoved his bloody arm trough the hole in the window and continued to push his way out. Her bones ached as she managed to stand up. Her body was giving out. She took a few steps forward, waiting to confront the man. He pulled his arm back through the splintered glass, smiled through the hole, and grabbed the knife from the floor. He threw himself at the window, shattered it completely, and landed on the road. His bloody hand wildly swung the knife from left to right as he lifted himself up onto his feet. Riley backed away and pulled off her jacket. The man looked ecstatic and charged her way. He swung the blade down toward her breast, but she shielded herself with her scrunched up coat. He forced the knife into the jacket and Riley took advantage of the situation. She grabbed the end of the blade with her coat and pulled it away from the man. She back away as she grabbed the knife, and then she charged. With one swing, Riley jabbed the weapon through his right temple. The man's eyes widened. His body dropped onto the cement road.

"I killed someone. I killed someone." Riley repeated herself aloud in shock. She knew that it was only for self-defence, but he would have never seen it coming. He could have a beautiful family back at home. He could have been a gentle person before the demon had chosen to possess him. She bowed her head with sorrow and pulled his body into some bushes as the rain began to fall. Riley looked deep into the forest in the direction the shadow had run. She could not help but picture the cloaked demon finishing him off. She knew the gentle terror had probably suffered the same fate as the hat-man.

Chapter 6

◊ ◊ ◊

For Riley, life seemed to be dying. She had lost something – something that left a large emptiness on the inside. Everything had become dark, and life felt meaningless. Riley felt no fear of death; she sped down the road toward Georgia Park faster then she had ever gone. The world could go to hell.

"Riley," echoed the whisper of a man. She looked in every direction, searching for the source of the voice. No one was around, but this did not surprise her. She stopped the cab behind her car and got out. Sunlight peered through a gap in the clouds. It felt nice on her skin; however, the park did not look as beautiful as it had before. The trees were losing colour, and patches of grass were missing everywhere.

She walked weakly over to her silver sedan and pulled the driver's door open. She looked over at Craig's red truck. It was still parked a short distance down the road. A burning anger boiled inside of her. She could feel hatred in every inch of her body – hatred for herself and for the man who told her she was crazy. Suddenly, Kevin O'Connor seemed unimportant. The demon was still lurking in the woods, and it had tried to kill her. Whether or not the murders were his, the demon would probably come back after her because she had saved Parker's life.

Riley stood with the door wide open and let the cool breeze flow through her hair. Thoughts about life, death, ghosts, and demons raced through her mind. She was so unsure of what the future would hold. A familiar sensation came upon her thoughts. She felt a light and heart-warming feeling. Her mind cleared itself of all of her life's stresses, and she could clearly hear a young man's voice speak in her subconscious. He whispered in her thoughts. *In the secret hideaway, forever they've kept them. Seek out their devil, and protect him.* A light echo followed the words that he spoke. She turned to stare deep into the forest across from the little wooden bridge; the demon had been there the entire time. Riley figured the demon would hide until someone like Craig would get close. Once anyone got close, however, it would be too late for them.

A fire, which Riley had never felt, burned in her stomach. Her eyes lit up with rage and fists formed from her hands. She jumped into her car and slammed the door shut. Her cell phone began to vibrate. She picked it up out of the cup holder and viewed a new message from her mother: *Okay, that's alright.* She closed the message and rolled her eyes.

She had one voicemail message. She selected it and listened. "Riley! My number one photographer! Where are you? I tried your house, but there was no answer." It was a rough, happy, older voice. "We may be on to something, superstar. As you may have noticed, my sister's paper told the public about the strange death of that hobo down in Fallsdale or somewhere. Anyways, there was another one just last night in Georgia; some loser and his two girlfriends decided to go to the park and he got himself killed by something. One of the two survivors is in the Fredsfurd Hospital. Be there with your camera at noon today when Jake interviews her," he said.

Riley set the phone back down in the cup holder. There was a heavy pressure in her chest. She could not believe what she had just heard. She gripped the steering wheel and tried to clear her mind. In desperation, she even hoped for a voice or a shadow to tell her what to do, but nothing happened.

She turned on her car and drove back toward Fallsdale. She had no clue as to what she was doing. She drove at full speed down the road, passing the exact spot into which she had dragged the Indian man. The day was warming up, and her car smelled of must. Her bloody hands stuck to the steering wheel as she drove, and the thought of the demon hovering around the forest next to her continuously repeated in her mind.

Back on Wrigley Lane, Riley remembered the hat-man from the night before. She suddenly felt more alone. He had frightened off the demon after it had killed Craig. *Craig.* She pulled up to her house. It had been almost a year since she had spoken to Craig before the news of his wedding. She opened the car door and jumped out. Charlie, her boss, would soon be waiting for her, but she could not care less. She walked up to the usually unlocked door, opened it, and gasped at the horrific sight before her.

Across the main hall, at the entrance to the kitchen, was the thick, brown, smoke-like being on all fours. Underneath his wildcat arched body was the demon. It looked completely paralyzed beneath the smoke. The brown figure seemed to be eating the demon. Its mouth, however, was in a different position than it had been the last time she saw it. The teeth of the brown figure were higher up on its face. The creature sucked in a black smoke that came out of the demon and continued doing so until the demon completely disappeared.

Riley stared wildly at the brown smoke for a moment. She was not certain whether she should be happy to see the demon dead or be afraid of the brown figure that killed it. She breathed heavily at the entrance, and the creature noticed her. Still on all fours, it tilted its head to the left and slowly stepped closer. Riley braced herself for escape, but the smoky being began to make a comfortable purring sound as it came even closer. If it had eyes, they would have been staring into hers. The creature's mouth had completely disappeared. Riley stepped backward as the being crawled right up to her. She stood quietly, keeping her head high as he stood himself up on his two hind legs. He stood at her exact height and leaned in closer to her face. The creature was only an inch away and seemed to be examining her without the use of eyes. Suddenly, two thin, long, diagonal slits appeared where a nose would have been. The width of the cuts extended and retracted repeatedly as it made a sniffing sound. The two holes abruptly closed, and the creature backed up a foot. He pointed a long, sharp, brown, and smoke-like finger toward her and poked her breast. He jumped backward in shock before coming closer to touch her face. Riley stood calmly and was surprised at how solid his hand felt. She let him examine her pointy nose. He traced her eyebrows. He seemed to stare at Riley for a moment before grabbing her hand with the two of his and placing it against his featureless face.

As smoky as the creature appeared, he was actually as solid and dry as any regular person. Riley brought her second hand up to feel his forehead and dragged them both to the temples on either side. As she held his head, two darker patches of smoke began to form eyes on the otherwise featureless face. The staring eyes frightened Riley into stepping backward and letting go of his face. As she let go, the eyes disappeared, followed by the whole figure. The phone began to ring. Riley waved her arms through the empty air, but she caught nothing solid. On the third ring, she answered.

"Hello?"

"Riley! Where the hell are you?" answered the rough and angry voice of Charlie Conrad.

"Well I'm answering my home phone," she said sarcastically.

"Don't be smart with me. Now get up here! This is great! Wait till you hear what this woman is saying!" he said excitedly.

That's when it struck Riley – with Charlie and the rest of the crew with him, what would Parker say? She hung up the phone, shut the door on her way out, and jumped back into the car. She tore down streets for the hospital, where Parker would be making a fool of herself.

Riley tapped her fingers repeatedly on the steering wheel as she waited at the stop lights. She was still a couple of blocks from the hospital. She could not believe she had let Charlie speak to Parker. Finally, the light turned green, but the cars ahead still were not moving. "Oh my god," she said to herself. She honked her horn a few times before the line up of vehicles began to advance. The car made it past the lights just as they had turned yellow.

She drove up onto the quiet road by the hospital and parked directly in front of the entrance. She hopped out onto the paved ground, slammed the door shut, and ran in.

Riley dashed through the hallways, up the carpeted stairs, and toward section J to room 26. She pushed open the door and bumped into the peach-haired woman, who glared at her and looked back to a small group of people who had all been giggling.

"You're very late," said a tall, grey-haired man in beige trousers and a dark blue dress shirt.

"I never got your message, Charlie," Riley lied as she walked past the peach-haired woman.

"And look at this – no camera," he said, pointing at her empty hands. "And you're very unattractive with that messy hair and no makeup. Go pretty yourself up somewhere. I've already got Jimmy taking photos." He pointed at a short, skinny man with large glasses and short black hair.

Riley glared at Charlie for a moment then pushed him out of her way as she went over to see Parker.

"Whoa there, that was very disrespectful," said Charlie.

"Suck it, Charlie," she said while looking back at him. Riley turned to Parker, who seemed frustrated beyond belief.

"Well, since you're not leaving," said Charlie embarrassingly, "You should hear what she has to say."

"Parker, what did you tell him?" asked Riley, completely ignoring Charlie.

"I just told him about that ghost thing – how it gave me these scratches. They won't believe me even though I showed them. But you were there so you could..."

"Who's your dealer?" Jimmy laughed while capturing a picture.

"Wait. You were with her? You're the Riley character. And this whole time I've been listening to this nutcase," said Charlie.

"Parker, don't say a thing," Riley hissed.

"Riley, I don't like the attitude you're giving me. You keep it up and I'll fire you."

"Don't have to – I quit!" she snapped at Charlie.

"Yeah right, because you'll find another chance like this," he said in a self-satisfied tone.

"I don't need to look. I've already got one – your sister, Charlie," she said, making Jimmy snicker.

Charlie's arrogant smile vanished from his face. "You're the unknown photographer," he said angrily. "That's why Kimberly always smirks," he added to himself.

Riley ignored him and bent back down to Parker. "It's gone," she whispered.

"Hey Orel, how long have you been working for her?" hissed Charlie.

Parker's eyes widened. "What do you mean?" she asked Riley quietly.

"The demon is dead," Riley whispered, still ignoring Charlie, who hissed at his team of men as they laughed.

"I can't explain right now," said Riley, turning away. "You," she said pointing at the little fat lady with peach coloured hair. "I thought she wasn't well enough for visitors? Get them out of here," she hissed.

The little, fat lady seemed insulted, but she did explain to Charlie and his two workers that they should leave. As expected, Jake – an unusually tall and lanky man with short light brown hair – was not happy to be leaving. He argued with the peach-haired woman while Jimmy wildly captured pictures of Parker with his camera and repeated "Smile!" Three young nurses had to join the peach-haired woman to help shut the men out of the room.

"Pigs," Riley spat.

After a long silence, Parker sat up in her nursing bed and unburied her face from her hands. She looked over to Riley, who sat in the burgundy chair next to her. They both stared at each other weakly.

"So, you killed it?" Parker asked, breaking the silence.

"No, but something did," Riley said as she looked away from Parker's wild gaze. After another moment of silence Riley said, "It's in my house."

Parker jerked herself slightly upwards at the sound of those words. "It's in your house?" she hissed in a whisper.

"No! Well, it's not anymore. A smoky thing that kind of looks human is there. I don't know. It just ate the demon," she explained.

"Ok, look." Parker said seriously. "Do you know what happened last night? What were you doing there?"

Parker had been there on the night of Craig's death. She had seen everything – even more then Riley had. She had been the one attacked by the demon that wandered the forest. And so, Riley explained everything – from her first nightmare of the demon in the forest, to the hat-man that Parker had seen at the park, and all the way up to the possessed cab driver. Parker listened, horrified at the details, and she could not help but wonder why Riley would be in the middle of all this. After what seemed like hours of discussion, Parker was caught up.

"Too bad the priest thought you were crazy," said Parker glumly. She buried her face back down into her pillow.

"Wait a sec," said Riley, noticing the wounds on Parker's back. Riley stood up and pulled the bib carefully apart. There were still three blue scratches with fiery edges, which slanted across Parker's back diagonally. But what was most curious, was that the cuts seemed to have healed into dark blue scar tissue. Parker tried swinging her head backward to see what Riley was looking at, but she could not bend far enough. "Weird," Riley said to herself.

"What?" asked Parker, trying to glance backward a second time.

"Nothing, it's fine," she said, touching the centre fire-edged mark.

Parker flipped herself back over and sat up straight. "It doesn't hurt anymore," she said. She stretched and slid off the nursing bed. "But I feel funny." She extended her legs and made her way to the cupboard across from the nursing bed. Parker opened the double door cabinet and pulled out some folded clothes. Parker left the room with the folded clothes, leaving Riley sitting in the burgundy chair. Upon returning, Riley noticed that Parker had put on the exact outfit from yesterday. It looked like someone had washed the clothes for her. She wore a grey, ripped long sleeve shirt that now had three long cut-outs on the back. The shirt was matched with a pair of dark, torn jeans. Riley was awestruck by Parker's quick change in physical appearance; her hair was long, smooth, and shiny, and it appeared as though she was wearing makeup. "You coming?" she asked Riley, who seemed confused.

"What? Uh, how'd you get ready so fast?"

"I don't know. I'm just fast," she answered in a strangely happy tone as she walked out.

Riley followed after her. "You're allowed out?" she asked, trying to keep up with Parker's pace.

Parker stopped dead in her tracks and turned to Riley. "Well I should be. There's nothing wrong with me; you said so yourself," she said rudely. Parker smiled and began to walk toward the large red doors at the end of the hallway.

"Yeah because Parker, I'm a doctor," Riley replied sarcastically as she followed behind. "What's wrong with you?"

Parker stopped. "What's wrong with me?" she spat into Riley's face. I'm not the one who can see into the future." She opened the doors and charged down the stairs.

The doors swung shut, but Riley flung them back open. "Your husband just died!" Riley shouted from the top of the staircase.

Parker turned and stared up at her. "No. My fiancée died," she said in a matter-of-fact tone. Parker smiled at Riley and began to walk away. Riley could not believe this ugly transformation. She charged down the stairs, grabbed the back of Parker's hair, and pulled hard. Parker yelped and turned toward Riley with an evil glare. Riley raised her right hand and slapped the redhead across the face. Parker gasped and rubbed the pinching red mark Riley's hand had left.

Riley's fiery eyes stared deep into Parker's. Parker seemed to have become weak once again and slowly walked away. Riley watched her heading for the main entrance and followed.

Parker stopped by the automatic doors. A young, brown-eyed nurse with long blonde hair stopped her. "You should go back to bed, Miss White," said the nurse. Parker turned her way with a pleading expression on her face. The nurse suddenly shrugged her shoulders. "Never mind, you look fine. As long as you're with someone you can go." Riley's mouth pursed, and her nose crinkled; Parker was not well at all. Riley looked around and hoped that someone would come to escort Parker back to her room. Riley had no sympathy for how long Parker would have to stay. No one was coming; the blonde nurse returned to her conversation with the secretary behind the thick sheet of glass, and the doctors were not anywhere to be seen. Her eyes rolled at the sight of Parker, who seemed to be debating on whether or not to break into the silver car that was parked by the automatic doors.

Parker stood against the car, apparently having come to her senses about whether or not she should enter it without permission. "It's mine," Riley said, glaring at Parker.

Parker looked away. "I need a ride home," she said. Riley rolled her eyes. "Please," Parker added weakly and stumbled closer to Riley.

Riley looked at her for a moment then nodded her head toward the car. Parker innocently got in, while Riley walked around toward the driver's side. She jumped in and turned the key.

"Where do you live?" asked Riley angrily.

"Two minutes from the Holy Cross Church."

Riley looked at Parker. Parker tried to ignore her. "Last night, I said I needed you to do something with me and you agreed," Riley said.

"I don't remember that."

"You're coming to the church with me," she said as she stomped on the gas pedal and drove off.

The car ride was long. They hit every red light along the way. Parker seemed tense and very uncomfortable in the passenger seat. She continuously looked over to Riley as though she was being held hostage. Riley, on the other hand, seemed determined. She kept her eyes on the road the entire time without giving a glance at Parker, who sat fidgeting in her seat. Riley occasionally smacked her fists against the wheel and cursed when they had to stop at a red light. Eventually, they found themselves back in Fallsdale.

Riley breathed heavily from behind the wheel as she slowly

pulled into the church parking lot. She looked over to Parker as she stopped the car. There was definite fear in Parker's eyes. Parker was sitting up straight and staring into the palms of her hands. "I didn't mean to, Riley," she cried. "I loved him."

"C'mon Parker, we'll just be a second," said Riley, sounding annoyed.

"But what are we doing?" she pleaded.

"I just need to prove to that priest that what I saw was real. Okay?" Parker nodded and slammed the door shut. She wiped away her tears and composed herself.

The two women stuck together as they entered the church and headed straight through the sanctuary. Riley looked around, but she could not see the priest anywhere. "Sir!" called out Riley as Monsignor entered from the back of the room. He noticed the two women and began to walk toward them with open arms. "How can I help you both?" he asked happily. The Priest directed his attention toward Parker as he continued getting closer. "Excited for the big day Miss White – or should I say—" Smack! Riley cut him off with a slap across the face. Parker covered her mouth as she gasped.

"Miss Orel!" He grasped at his cheek. "This is some unacceptable behaviour – and in the house of God!"

"Oh, you and your God can go—"

"No!" shouted Parker. "Riley, not here," she begged weakly.

"Parker, if it weren't for him, Craig would still be alive!" she hissed

"Craig would have died either way," said the priest as he rolled his eyes.

Riley looked at him as though in shock. "So you believed me the whole time. You monster! I told you that someone was about to die, and you did nothing," she screamed.

"Nothing could have been done; you had already seen his death," he said calmly.

"But Parker lives," she said while pointing at the trembling redhead.

"Parker didn't die in your dream now, did she?" he said calmly.

"You know a lot about this stuff?" asked Riley.

"I've already told you, Miss Orel, that I have dealt with people like you before," he said with a smirk.

Riley's eyes sharpened and Parker came between the both of them. "Let's just go," she begged. She placed her both hands on Riley's shoulders to help keep her balance.

Riley looked at the priest behind Parker and noticed that he was trying to peer at her wounds through the cuts in her shirt. Riley glared at the man, who noticed her and quickly backed up a few feet.

"Those cuts on your back, Miss White, are they from Miss Orel's shadow creature?"

Parker turned slowly to face him. "Yeah," she said faintly.

"Interesting," he said as he turned and walked away.

"Listen, Father! You have to help us. The demon or 'shadow creature' has already possessed a man and sent him after Riley. Forgive her behaviour and help her, please," Parker begged with much strength as she could muster.

The old man stopped and seemed to ponder. "I'll do my best," he said as he left them without a second look.

Parker stood and watched the priest leave the room as Riley walked up beside her. Parker pinched the bridge of her nose. "I've got such a headache," she said. Riley shrugged her shoulders and gave a slight smirk.

The hatred Riley had felt for Parker at the hospital seemed to be lessening. She was pleased that Parker had tried getting help for their problem. "C'mon on, I'll drive you home," she said calmly.

Making their way to the main entrance, Riley noticed how slow and weak Parker appeared. "Are you alright?" she asked, but Parker kept quiet and continued to limp slightly as she walked. A moment later, Parker stopped. She began to pant. "I think I'll take you back to the hospital," Riley said worryingly.

Parker looked to the floor. "No."

"Parker..." Riley touched the redhead's forehead. "You're burning up."

"I'm always this warm," she said in a rather happy and energetic tone as she straightened up her posture. "I'm just very tired, and I want my own bed." Parker walked over to the two wooden doors and walked out.

Scenarios began to form in Riley's mind. *What if the demon did something to Parker when it gave her those wounds?* She could picture Parker turning into the shadow creature as she drove her home. She could imagine Parker trying to kill her just as the cab driver had tried. Riley's heart raced. She felt the urge to get away from Parker. She brushed her bangs away from her face and decided to make a run for it, but before she could turn around to leave through the back exit, Parker peeked in through the door curiously. Riley stared back into Parker's hazelnut eyes with uncertainty.

"Um, Riley?" Parker's lips began to tremble, and a tear slid down her face. "Craig has the key," she wept.

Riley's heart jerked; Parker could not be a monster. At that moment, Riley began to feel that sympathy she had been lacking for her almost-sister-in-law. She imagined that Parker was trying to hide the pain she truly felt for the loss of Craig – that her previously dismissive attitude was just a defence mechanism. Riley felt horrible, but she could not find any words to sooth Parker's heartbreak. She figured she might as well keep an eye on her. "Want some tea?" Riley asked.

Chapter 7

Riley stared at the now puffy-eyed, tangled-haired, and sobbing Parker as she pulled up onto the right side of the street across from her house. Parker was first to get out as she wiped away her tears while Riley continued to sit, contemplating what she might do with parker. *Maybe I'll let her stay the night or just somehow trick her back into the hospital.* It was not until she saw Parker crossing the street that Riley brushed her bangs out of her face and stepped out of the car.

She followed Parker up the cement walkway and onto the porch where she was waiting for Riley to unlock the door. "It's not locked," said Riley. She pushed the door open and let Parker in. "How did you know this was my place?" she asked Parker, who was peeking curiously into the dark living room.

"Craig showed me before," she said, but she quickly changed the subject when noticing the sad expression on Riley's face. Parker instead began to scold Riley for not locking her doors. To this, Riley shrugged her shoulders as she walked into the living room.

"I thought I opened these?" Riley said to herself while pulling open the brown curtains.

She looked over to Parker, who entered innocently, and her eyes sharpened. "What happened to you?" she said.

"What are you talking about?" Parker asked as she made a complete stop three feet into the room.

"Your hair and makeup – it was fine and then all of a sudden, you looked really sick in the car," she said perplexed.

"Thanks?" she said, brushing her now clean and fiery red hair back behind her ear.

Riley was stumped. She had seen Parker go from a flawless beauty to looking horribly sick and back. She wondered if she was seeing into the future or being given some sort of sign like she had been given in the dreams. Just as the thought of her dreams began to put her on edge, she jumped as her eyes caught it – the sight of the brown figure. It poked its head out from the side of the couch for a split second and hid back behind it again. Parker's eyes slowly followed Riley's gaze. "You alright?" she asked as she looked back toward Riley, who was looking around the couch for the apparition. The brown smoke-like being had gone.

"Riley, are you alright?" she asked nervously.

"It's alright. I just thought I saw something." She turned back to Parker. "Anyway, I'll go get the tea." She pointed at the living room doorway indicating the kitchen where her china set was. "You can sit down if you want. The remote is in the table drawer in front of you. You know, if you feel like watching anything. Yeah... that one," she said as Parker went through the drawer to find the remote.

Riley grabbed the coffee maker and shoved it underneath the sink into a light wooden cabinet. She pulled out the electric teapot and placed it next to the microwave and sink. Reaching over her head, she pulled two tea bags and china mugs out of the cabinet above. As the teapot warmed, she began to neatly place some store-bought oatmeal cookies on a tray. Beep! Beep! The teapot dinged signalling that the water had come to a boil and startling Riley's body into a jump. As her arms flew upward, she dropped three of the cookies onto the floor and began to shiver. *Settle down. Settle down.* Riley rubbed her head to try calming the shivering. She took deep breaths to slow the pace of her heart, but her stomach began to feel queasy, and she could not seem to compose herself. *It was only the–* BANG! Her thoughts were interrupted by a heavy thud from the living room. Mumbles and gasps sounded from the other room. Riley ran into the living room and was shocked by the scene before her: Parker was lying halfway off the sofa, prying the claws of the brown smoke-like being off of her mouth.

"Get off me!" Parker shouted as she succeeded at pushing him off just long enough to stand on her feet. The creature raised itself onto its hands and feet and looked ready to pounce. With a burst of courage and anger, Riley tackled him to the ground.

"What're you doing?" she yelled at him as she pushed him toward the ground to help herself up. The creature made no sound. It looked at Parker, bared its sharp teeth, and disappeared.

Riley stood still, brimming with anger and staring at the spot where the creature had disappeared from. "That's it?" asked Parker angrily. "That's the thing that killed the shadow demon?" Parker's eyes looked dark and intense. She was fidgeting like she did not know what to do with her hands until they formed firm fists. She was hysterical.

Riley could not believe she had thought the brown creature was not a danger to anyone. It had been her protector but was now something to be afraid of. She was ashamed with herself; he had attacked Parker for no reason. "Riley?" Parker sounded annoyed that Riley was not acknowledging her.

"Parker, you didn't give him a reason to do that, did you?" Riley asked, hopeful that Parker had instigated the struggle.

"What?" Parker was confused. "It just jumped out of nowhere and tried pinning me down. I was just turning on the TV!" Parker sat down on the sofa and rested her head in her hands. Minutes passed in silence. Riley stared at her from the spot where the brown creature had disappeared. "Riley, it scared me."

From then on, Parker followed Riley whenever she left the room. They went into the kitchen for their tea when Riley remembered the cooling teapot. At the wooden table, they sat uncomfortably. Parker was mentally stressed out. Riley noticed her eyes were wildly flying in every direction. She was always looking over her shoulder. Riley found herself a bit jealous of Parker's nervousness. *Who wouldn't have the same reaction? Only me. This is what my life has become. My fear has become my norm.* Riley peered into the main hall and glared at the brown smoke-like being, which had been poking his head through the doorway without Parker even noticing. *This is my life.*

Time crept away slowly. The creature eventually stopped making appearances behind Parker's back. Riley drew a breath. "So what's the plan?" she asked calmly as Parker sipped her tea and stared out of the kitchen window with a traumatized look.

"Hmm?" said Parker as she came back to her senses. "What do you mean?"

"Well, are you staying here the night or do you have somewhere to go, someone who can look after you?" she asked. Parker stared at her sadly. "You can sleep on the couch."

"No, no. I'm fine, Riley," she quickly interrupted. "I'll just have my mom pick me up, and she'll give me the extra key she has to my place." Parker shot Riley a fake, bubbly smile. Riley wanted to argue, but she figured she would just talk with Mrs. White about Parker needing a babysitter for a while.

Noticing the smoke-like being appear behind Parker for the seventh time, Riley said, "Maybe he did that because he didn't know you."

Parker followed Riley's unblinking gaze and jumped at the sight of the crouching shadow behind her. Unintelligible sounds screeched out of her mouth as she lost control of her body, jumped from her seat, and fell back against the fridge. Parker closed her eyes and braced herself for an attack. When nothing happened, she fearfully looked at Riley and back at the monster.

Riley's eyes were intensely fixed on the crouching shadow. Her head shook slightly for a moment, and she addressed the creature. "You don't do that." The cloudy being bowed its head and sat down. "He must have made a mistake." Her eyes met Parker's shocked and terrified expression. Parker was sprawled back against the refrigerator. Her legs were shaking too hard to help prop herself up. "Parker, it's ok now. You can trust me." Parker said nothing, but she started breathing at a more normal pace. Riley let her catch her breath before asking, "Do you want to see him?"

"You nuts? Riley, that pecker is gonna kill someone. It's gonna kill us!" she hissed.

Riley glared at her for a moment. "He's not going to hurt you. He knows he did something bad." She looked back at the sitting figure in the hallway.

"Yeah? If it can take out a shadow creature in one bite, don't you think it's dangerous? And sorry if I don't forgive it for trying to tear me to shreds!" she screamed.

"C'mon over here, you pecker-head!" Riley smirked at the cowering Parker and stretched out a hand toward the shadow-like being. "C'mon Peck. Good job, Parker," Riley smiled. "You found his name."

A smoky hand crossed over into the kitchen and made Parker tighten up even more. "Yes, yes," Parker said sarcastically. "Let's dub him 'Pecker-Head,' hit him over the head with a bottle, and while he's knocked out, ditch him somewhere!"

"No Parker – Peck." Riley lowered herself to the floor and motioned for Peck to come. Peck crawled into the kitchen on all fours and stared at Parker, who still breathed heavily. He made his way toward Riley and sat beside her. She could not remember ever feeling as excited to be in the presence of the thick, brown smoke-like being. She pet the top of his remarkably solid head and smiled. *My protector has returned.* Riley looked up at Parker. "Wanna see him?" she asked.

"I can see fine from here," she said in a shaky voice.

Riley stared at Peck, and she watched him face Parker curiously. His index finger scratched a white ceramic floor tile as a growling sound erupted from his throat. Riley immediately grabbed hold of his head with her hands and directed his attention at herself. She shook her head with a glare in her eyes, and two black glimmering eyes appeared upon his face. The dark eyes glared back at her before quickly disappearing. Peck looked away from them. Riley, being slightly unsettled, by his display of anger toward her, shifted backward on her knees while taking her hands off him. At that moment, a beautiful red cardinal rested itself upon the kitchen window sill and lightly tapped the glass. Peck hissed at the bird through clenched teeth before disappearing again.

"Wow," Riley said with wide eyes. "I guess it's a sign, right?" she smirked at Parker, who loosened away from the fridge. "Peck it is! Watch it, there might be some glass on the floor somewhere around there," she added after noticing Parker hesitatingly leaving her corner.

"I don't see any," she said while stepping cautiously toward one of the kitchen chairs. Parker waved her arms through the air, in fear of running into Peck. Riley stood up as Parker seated herself and began to sip her cold tea. "Why doesn't he hurt you?" Parker asked grumpily.

"I don't know."

Parker sipped her tea. "Well I mean, did you see how insulted he looked when you pushed him over in the living room?" Parker looked across the table at Riley.

"I think he's just used to me." Riley looked longingly into the empty hallway. "And if that's the case, then I'd give it a day for him to start liking you." A long silence followed her words. *Why would anyone want to be a part of this? Why would anyone else want to give it a day for this to become their norm?* Parker sipped her tea and looked behind herself every few minutes, fearing that Peck would soon try to attack again. Riley sat with her elbows propped up on the table and munched on a strawberry jam cookie.

Riley dipped her cookies in her tea, and Parker finally broke the silence. "So what's with you and the priest?" Riley's nose crinkled as she placed her mug on the table.

"I don't know. Like, he said he knew about this kind of stuff." She shrugged her shoulders and shook her head in anger. "It has to be possible that I can change what I see in the dreams or else what's the point in seeing them, right?" she asked, pushing her bangs behind her ear.

"Well, you saved me," said Parker in a reassuring tone.

"You would have lived anyway. I didn't see you die in the dream." Riley gulped down the rest of her tea.

"But maybe that's because you were there. I mean, you were always supposed to be there, right? Maybe your purpose was to distract the shadow creature long enough for the hat-man to chase it away. Maybe if you wouldn't have shown up, I would have died before the demon fled."

Parker's theory lifted Riley's spirits as much as they could be lifted, but she still did not understand why the hat-man could not have stopped the shadow creature sooner. Parker could not think of any good explanation either. They sat quietly, each lost in their own thoughts, and each hoping for a reason that Craig's death was unavoidable. Their comfort never came.

Parker gulped back the last of her tea and watched the red cardinal on the window sill. The little bird was watching her. It tilted its head for a moment then took off. Parker grabbed a cookie and ate while Riley brought the two mugs over to the sink.

"Hey so, are you sure..." Riley turned and stopped when she noticed Parker swaying from side to side in her seat. "Parker? Are you sure you want..." Riley took a step closer to Parker. "Are you ok?"

"Hmm? Yeah, are you ok?" She asked once back to her senses.

"Yeah."

"I'm feeling a little tired, I guess. I should call my mom." Parker grabbed at her forehead. "Oh god, my head hurts so much." As Parker stumbled off her chair, Riley thought she actually seemed intoxicated.

"Parker, I think you should sit."

"No, I think I should sleep," she said, and she walked into the living room leaving Riley standing in the kitchen.

Riley followed after Parker and found her already lost in a deep sleep on the dark blue couch.

Chapter 8

Her blonde hair flew in her face, and her arms swung at full speed as she ran deeper into the forest. It was catching up to her. She could feel its beady, black eyes watching her as the ground began to tremble. Through the corner of her eye, she saw its hairy arm reach for her. *It's over.* Her heart was pounding so hard that she was sure it was on the verge of bursting. *I have to slow down.*

Riley woke up with a start. She was lying in her bed as Parker occupied the living room loveseat. Her panting breath settled as she slipped out of bed. She walked barefoot across the cold wooden floor in her sweaty stripped pyjama pants and white T-shirt. With wet bangs plastered across her forehead, she examined her appearance in the bathroom mirror. Her trembling hand turned on the faucet, and she wiped down her face with a wet wash cloth from the drawer beneath the sink.

The black eyes continued to blink in her imagination each time she closed her eyes. Her arm continued to feel the grip of the hairy hand that grabbed her. She drew a deep breath and noticed through her peripheral vision that Peck had decided to make another appearance. He was poking his head innocently into the bathroom from the doorway behind her. Something about the way he looked made her feel uneasy. He walked into the bathroom on two legs and tilted his head while looking at her. Riley's body tightened and instinctively darted itself through the doorway, into the hall, through the kitchen, and back into the living room where she found parker sitting on the couch with the lamp on by her side.

They stared at each other as Riley drew a breath of relief. "What are you doing up? It's like two in the morning," she said as she walked into the dimly lit room.

"Oh, I was sleeping," she said wide-eyed. "But then, I started feeling really warm, and when I got up to turn on the light, he was standing in the doorway just watching me." Parker pointed at Peck, who made his way back under the arch of the doorway.

Riley watched Peck for a moment. "He didn't come near you or anything, right?" she asked hopefully.

"Oh. No. He ran away and must have gone to get you up."

"He was just standing behind me," she reassured Parker. "No, what really woke me was another nightmare. But it was just the normal type of nightmare that normal people have." She smiled at Parker for a moment and yawned.

Parker on the other hand, was sceptical about the possibility of Riley's nightmare being at all normal. After convincing Riley to tell her about the dream, she mumbled, "I mean, just think about it for a sec. If there are such things as shadow creatures, faceless hat-men, and Peck, then maybe this forest monster is a real thing too." Parker's theory did nothing but put Riley into a disgruntled state. She walked over, dropped onto the loveseat, and sat with her arms crossed. Riley understood why she was angry – Parker was possibly right, and she did not want to believe it. She longed for at least one normal dream. It was something she feared would never happen again.

"Is he alright?" asked Parker, nodding to Peck. Riley shrugged and shuffled to get comfortable. Parker was right to ask the question; Peck was not acting much like his usual curious and childlike self.

He leaned stiffly against the doorway and stared at Riley. His cloudy body eventually mimicked a sighing motion without actually releasing any sound.

"I think he is," she said while staring at him. "Peck, you alright?" she asked. Riley stood up to check on him, but he had disappeared.

"Wow, I'm not sure. I think you're right about him though. I mean, he must have just needed to understand that I wasn't going to hurt either of you," Parker said as Riley sat back down, "I think that's what made him so uncomfortable with me." She yawned sleepily while resting against the couch cushions.

Riley stared at the empty doorway Peck had left behind. "Parker, what if you're right about the monster in the forest?" Her voice shook slightly.

Parker sat up, crossed her legs, and looked at Riley. "Then I guess we'll just have to stop it. Or it could be possible that it's a good monster, right?"

Riley sat quietly for a moment without moving, her eyes looking weak and her breathing gaining speed. "It grabbed me," she said in a whisper.

"What?" Parker leaned toward her.

"It grabbed me with one hand," she said worryingly.

Riley slumped back into the cushions of the loveseat, and Parker mimicked her movements on the other side of the couch. They sat in silence until Parker drifted away into a deep sleep. Riley, however, sat wide-eyed for hours until sleep eventually began to catch up with her, and she moved into her bedroom. She could not stop worrying about the dark, hairy hand that might one day kill her.

The sun crept through Riley's uncovered bedroom window a few hours later. She stretched out of bed and wandered into the bathroom to wash up. Pushing aside the curtains of the small bathroom window, she turned to face the mirror as she scrubbed her teeth with a blue toothbrush. After a needed rinse, she was ready for breakfast.

The kitchen tiles were so cold on her bare feet, but on a groggy morning like this, the prospect of a jolting cup of coffee was worth the chill. As she poured the strong smelling grinds into the coffee maker, Parker drowsily walked into the kitchen.

"I'm so tired," she managed to blurt out in a half-yawn and grabbed a chair facing Riley. "Those look good." Parker eyed the pastries Riley had thrown into the oven that were now cooling off on the countertop.

"You know, I don't understand how if you don't sleep, you get tired, and if you sleep a little more than usual, you're still tired," Riley said, and she pulled up a chair opposite from Parker. "Coffee will be ready soon. You want some?"

"Yeah. Thanks." Parker smiled sweetly back at Riley and stretched her arms up over her head.

They downed their pastries and coffee in silence – their bodies grateful to feel refuelled. Riley stared at the wall as she chewed. She could not take her mind off of the nightmare monster with the black eyes. The dream replayed in her memory over and over. She remembered the feeling of being terrified and alone. She had been panting and was looking for something, but she could not remember what it was. Suddenly, branches broke, and she saw the hairy beast's eyes watching her as she ran. She ran as fast as she could until she gave up.

Riley was so angry that she had stopped running and let the forest beast catch her. *Why didn't I try harder? I could have ducked into a bush or screamed louder. I just gave up. Doesn't matter – this won't happen. It won't ever happen.* Riley convinced herself that all she had to do was stay out of the forest, and she would never have to face whatever monster may be hiding deep within.

"I'm so sorry, Riley," said Parker after noticing Riley's worried expression. "I honestly didn't want to fall asleep last night. It just happened."

"Parker, that's no problem. I invited you to stay last night, right?" she said with a smirk.

Parker nodded and finished up her food before going to the bathroom to wash up. In just a couple minutes, Parker had time to obtain perfect hair and flawless skin. Riley washed a few dishes and shoved the coffee machine back underneath the sink. "How the hell do you get ready so quickly?" Riley asked as she left the room to find a pair of clean clothes.

Riley dived into the piles of laundry on the floor by her bed in search of something clean to wear. Laundry was not her speciality. She pulled on a new pair of jeans and an amazingly unwrinkled yellow shirt with a diagonal red stripe that travelled from her right shoulder to the hem at the bottom left.

Riley entered the kitchen where Parker sat watching a beautiful red cardinal that was perched on the window sill. "So now with the shadow creature gone," said Parker after coming out of her trance, "what happens? Does that beast in the forest have to be killed by Peck too?"

"No!" said Riley hastily. "I just won't go into a forest for the rest of my life – or not until I'm older – my hands weren't wrinkled in the dream." Stressed out, Riley sat down at the table.

"Well, remember what the priest said about the dreams?" Parker crossed her arms in a serious fashion. "He said that if it happens in the dreams, then it will happen in real life."

Parker slumped against the back of her chair and stared at the red cardinal. Riley knew Parker was worried about what the priest had said because of the way the reality of the dreams had turned Craig from a brother and fiancé into a corpse. *Oh god, Craig.* Nausea hit Riley like a brick wall. *My brother is never coming back.* If this new nightmare came true, Parker would be completely alone in this madness.

As they sat at the table, Peck continued to poke his head in and out from around the corner. Riley stared at the wall, waiting to see him again. Her eyes widened as a man's voice boomed inside her head, blocking out any noise from her real surroundings. *In the secret hideaway, forever they've kept them. Seek out their devil, and protect him.* Riley sprung up on her feet to check every corner of the room for Peck.

"Are you alright? What's going on?" Parker asked anxiously and turned back to Riley with wide eyes.

"I'm hearing things."

"What?"

"In the secret hideaway, forever they've kept them. Seek out their devil, and protect him. What does this mean? What does this mean?" Riley paced around the kitchen, and looked at Parker, hoping for an explanation.

Parker was at a loss for words. "Um… what?"

"This voice – it just keeps repeating those words," she said through the spaces between her fingers. "I don't know. Ever since I noticed that something was up with these stupid dreams I've been having, a man's voice has been speaking to me – kind of."

"Kind of?" Parker asked.

"I've heard the voices of many people, but that was kind of in a dream. This other voice, I hear when I'm awake. He keeps telling me to find a devil."

"Daydream?" said Parker as she watched the cardinal fly away.

Riley wiped her eyes of the sleep collecting in their corners. Her eyes glared at the bedroom hallway as Peck reappeared.

"I know it sounds crazy," Riley added, "but you've seen these things come to life. Parker, they're in my head."

"Riley, I don't think you're crazy, but you have to understand that this is scaring me. It's scaring me a lot." Parker's eyes began to water, and her bottom lip quivered as she spoke. "All me and Craig wanted to do was go back to the bike path. Last summer, I was riding my bike along that path in the park, and a man rode up on his bike behind me. He was so nice. We talked and joked as we came up to the hills. It was Craig." Riley saw a tear attempting to escape from Parker's eye. "We began to see each other at the coffee pub on Wrigley where I worked before the diner opened. Everything was so perfect and fun. He made me feel so light-hearted. I can't believe this actually happened. A monster killed him in front of me."

Riley watched the tear slide down Parker's cheek. Her heart jerked, and she noticed that Peck was leaning up against the wall by the kitchen doorway. He watched Riley carefully. She was at a loss for words, and she could not handle thinking about her dead brother, so Riley focused on her new pet instead. *Parker is right. There's something strange about Peck – strange even for a supernatural being.* Peck's body filled up as if he had taken a deep breath and then deflated again. His shoulders slouched over as if he was sighing. He disappeared.

"And now there's another beast out there to kill us," said Parker. Riley felt as though she had probably been tuning out her almost sister-in-law. Parker's face was red and covered in tears.

"That beast grabs me, not you," Riley said angrily.

"Just because you didn't see it in your dream, doesn't mean it's not going to happen," Parker choked out.

"Well, you weren't there," Riley hissed.

"Cause I was dead."

"Parker!" Riley snapped. "It doesn't matter! I'm not going into any forests any time soon."

"That's what you think. What if something leads you into it? What if something forces you there?"

As they argued, a tapping noise came from the window, and

they both turned instinctively. The red cardinal had come back and pecked at the window before flying away again. Riley's eyes rolled as she turned back to Parker.

"Well, I guess the bird wants us to stop," smirked Parker. "I'm gonna see if I can get the key from my mom."

"The phone's right there!" Riley pointed at the cordless phone hanging on the wall in its charger.

"Thanks," Parker said as she walked over to the telephone to call her mother. Riley listened in to Parker's short responses to her mother, who obviously carried the conversation. "Hello. Yeah it's me. Yeah I'm – oh they called you?" Tears emerged from Parker's puffy eyes. "Mom, I miss him," she whimpered. "Can you pick me up? Oh, I didn't know. Yeah, but mom the nurse said I looked good enough to leave with Riley. She's his step sister... yes that one," Parker hissed and sniffed. "I'm at 442 Diligent. Thanks and can you bring me your spare key? Bye, I love you." Parker hung up the phone and tried to hide her face as she cleaned up her tears.

"She'll be here soon," she told Riley.

Riley stared at her, her eyebrow raised. "That one?" she asked.

"Oh, Riley," said Parker, annoyed.

"I didn't know there were more sisters," Riley hissed.

"No, it's nothing."

Riley watched Parker, who stood behind the chair opposite of her. "Yeah, it is fine, I just want to know how everyone talks about me," she said and crossed her arms.

"You were just never around, that's all," Parker said.

Riley recalled her mother basically telling her once that no one liked her. "You know what? I don't get along with Tim, alright?" Riley puffed and stood from her seat, making Parker flinch. "I just don't. So to avoid conflict for everyone else, I'm barely around." Riley shrugged and shook her head. "I stay out of everyone's way to make things more peaceful for them, and yet they still talk about me behind my back."

Riley looked away for a moment then back at Parker with glaring eyes. "Honestly, they only know me from his point of view, Parker! I've never met anyone from your family, yet somehow they know me as this horrible person. It's not fair!" Riley looked pleadingly at Parker before becoming somewhat embarrassed about her emotional revelation and disappearing to her room to compose herself. After a few minutes of methodical breathing, she returned to Parker's company.

"Riley," squeaked Parker as someone knocked on the front door.

"You know what?" said Riley with a smirk. "To hell with it – if, they're gonna think of me like that…" Riley stormed out of the room without finishing her thought with a concernedly large grin forming across her face.

Parker ran after her into the main hallway as Riley opened with, to Parker's relief, a believable smile. The door swung open revealing a beautiful, thin, dark-haired woman wearing black-rimmed glasses. Gorgeous hazel-nut eyes shone out from behind them. Parker stood at her height, and they shared the same skin tone, but beside that, Riley could not see any of Mrs. White in Parker.

"Hello," greeted Riley in a kind tone.

The woman behind the black glasses looked at Riley as though she was shocked to find that maybe Riley was not such a monster. She smiled pityingly back at Riley and extended her hand.

"Lana White," she said, shaking Riley's hand. Lana then turned to Parker to hug her tightly. "Oh I'm so sorry, Bay!" She patted her daughter on the back. Her head, tight against Parker's shoulder, turned to Riley with teary eyes. "I'm very sorry," she said.

Riley's fake smile twitched as she drew a deep breath. She nodded at Parker's mother, but could not say a word. Parker sniffed as her mother ushered her out the door. "Thank you, Riley," she said halfway down the porch steps. Parker continued on her way to her mother's black sedan.

Riley smiled sweetly and nodded. She watched Parker hop into the car followed by her mother. A few minutes passed before they took off.

Riley's unease about the potential new monster was doubled by the fact that she kept wondering about the true fate of the shadow monster. *Could a monster like that even die? What if it comes back?* Something did not feel quite right in the pit of her stomach. She pictured waking up one night to find the cloaked ghost itself hovering into her bedroom as she slept. She could see its clenching, birdlike feet and its sharp, pale green hand.

Her deep breath quivered. She stared out the window from the couch while the television played commercials that were drowned out by her constant worrying. The house was clean. She had nothing to preoccupy herself with. *Maybe I should give someone a call and connect with real life. Charlie? That would be a waste. Kimberly? I was supposed to wait for her to contact me first.* For the last year, Riley had been craving this type of relaxed day; however, now that it was here, she no longer wanted it.

The cold summer's evening brought a drizzle of rain. On the edge of the couch, she sat, thinking about how everyone thought badly of her before even meeting her in person. Riley felt the room warm up as she thought about how she would force everyone to eat their words on the day they would meet. Most of all, she could not wait to prove Tim wrong. She wanted to be what Tim thought was perfect; her home would be clean and tidy, and she would work hard for her money and not procrastinate as she once did. She would be the coordinated and driven woman that Tim would have never expected.

She turned off the television set and retreated to the kitchen for super. She boiled chicken noodle soup on the stove and ate quietly at the table without any sight of Peck. Riley slurped her soup while absentmindedly twisting her bangs between her fingers. There was nothing else to do. Eventually, she saw Peck crawl into the main hall from the living room. She watched him as he circled by the door and occasionally growled.

"You need out?" she asked, leaning on the table.

Peck simply stopped to turn her way and growl before returning to his endless circling. Riley raised an eyebrow at the confusing creature. "Alrighty then," she said and made her way to the bedroom. For appearances, she stuffed piles of clothes underneath her bed and pulled the solid beige comforter neatly into place. She smiled and retired to the sofa in the living room to rest and watch television.

Peck remained prowling in the main hallway as Riley zoned out to a cooking show. He eventually came into the living room and circled around the window as he continued to growl. Riley looked at him, wide-eyed and half expecting to be attacked. She turned off the television. Peck's entire body froze still. His head tilted as if to listen from a different angle with his sharp ears. His head shot into the air as two long, diagonal slits appeared on his face that extended and retracted as he sniffed. He crouched down to the ground and crawled back into the hallway, still sniffing. It had happened so unexpectedly that Riley barely had time to feel frightened.

"Peck!" she called. She tried following him into the hallway, but he hissed back through a mouthful of sharp teeth. She backed away without another word.

The front door burst open at full force, throwing Peck backward. He attempted to jump at whoever was there; however, a dark, muscular arm came through and gripped his throat. Peck struggled to break free from the grip; he clawed at the arm and hissed fiercely but could not get away.

"Peck!" cried Riley as she hurdled herself at the tall man. "Let him go!" she screamed as she smacked the man in the face and struggled to push him over. "Disappear, Peck! Leave!" she yelled. Before Peck could obey, he fell silent and limp. The tall man set him down on the floor. The stranger was completely unaffected, as though he had not yet realized that Riley had been attempting to push him down.

"Riley Orel!" said a happy voice from outside the door. In walked a young man, just as dark skinned but much shorter than the other. The man who had gripped Peck was a good three inches taller than she was. This young man was an inch shorter than her. She guessed he was about 15 years old. Riley stared into his dark brown eyes while his companion left and re-entered with a cage for Peck. The young man smiled with beautiful white teeth as he looked back at her.

"How do you know me?" she hissed at him.

The young man rolled up his red, plaid shirtsleeves as he looked down at Peck, who now lay motionless in the cage. "We know everything," he said with a smile.

"How dare you break down my door and hurt him!" she hissed, nose to nose with the shorter of the two.

"Oh, you want it fixed?" He pointed at the door behind him with his thumb. "Rocky," he commanded to the taller and stronger looking man. His smile never faded.

Riley grabbed the boy from the scruff of his shirt, and Rocky put his hand menacingly on her shoulder. "It's alright," he said to Rocky, who let go and left the house through the entrance. "I'm Fang." He extended a hand between their almost touching noses. "Your Peck is fine. We just didn't want him hurting anyone, that's all," he said. "Really stupid things aren't they, shadow figures?" he said as he stared down at the metal cage.

Riley would not stand for it – these people just barging in and talking rudely about her protector. She swung a fist at Fang's face. It made contact but did not seem to faze him at all. He looked back at Riley and smiled as he grabbed both her wrists and held them together. Riley twisted and pulled but could not break from Fang's grip. His smile disgusted her. She spit in his face. With one arm, he pushed her to the ground and wiped the spit off his cheek with the other. Rocky came back in with a red toolbox and knelt on the ground as he fixed the door's hinge.

"Just so no one thinks you were taken by force," Fang sneered as Riley regained her balance on two feet.

"What do you mean?" she spat.

"I mean, you're going to come with us," he replied calmly as Rocky stood up behind him.

"No I'm not." Riley backed away.

"Riley, if you resist, my friend here," he pointed at Rocky, "will just have to persuade you."

Riley continued to back away as Rocky came forward. She spun around, jumped to her feet, and made a run for the back door but felt both of Rocky's hard arms close in around her stomach. "Hurry up, Rocky. Get her out of here before this thing wakes up, I don't want to hear it screech in pain." She lay over Rocky's shoulder, staring at the cage that was being left in the entrance. The door closed between herself and Peck. She was alone.

Riley screamed for help but no one came. She continued to kick and punch Rocky as he shoved her into a large black van. Fang, who had entered from the other side, began to pull her in. He was surprisingly strong for a boy. Refusing to give up, Riley gave him a kick in the face that made him fall backward against the door. Rocky grabbed her by the neck, in the same way he had grabbed Peck. He forced her to face him as he pushed her into the van. Fang tied her feet as Rocky shut the sliding door. She kept kicking and screaming as they bound her tighter. *This isn't happening! This has to be a nightmare! Oh god.* She panicked but could not wake herself. She thrashed around, hoping to startle herself into wakefulness or find some escape. As she tossed uncontrollably, Rocky grabbed and threw her over the seat into the back of the van where her spinning head knocked itself out on his red toolbox. Riley's vision faded.

Chapter 9

◊ ◊ ◊

Riley refused to stare at the beast that held her in its hands. She wanted to see it, but she was too scared. She fought hard to break free from its grip, but it was too strong. She screamed and pleaded to be let go. With her in its grip, the beast began to run away from something she felt she needed to protect. She needed to get back to it. Whatever she was missing was not far away and was alone, and she was alone with the beast.

Riley woke up to the face of a young brunette woman. She was as dark skinned as Fang and Rocky, and she dabbed at Riley's forehead with a warm cloth. Her big brown eyes caught Riley's, and she smiled sweetly before leaving the pale beige room through a dark wooden door on the left. Riley sat up in the single, white-sheeted bed and looked around at the two rows of identical beds lined up across the walls. Someone had changed her into a long white nightgown. She slid onto the cold hardwood floor and walked barefooted across the room to the wooden door.

Through the door, she walked out onto a dusty street filled with children and women who were standing and playing outside of dozens of identical mud huts. They wore tattered beige cloth for clothes. As Riley made an appearance on the road, the women stopped to stare at her.

She turned to look at the wooden cabin she had come from. A large hospital cross was carved on both sides of the dark wooden door. She turned back to the people on the road. Everyone watched her now, including the children. Eyes followed as she walked along the dirt path. A young child ran toward her with a pebble in hand, ready to throw. He was standing defensively at the end of the road which led to his hut. A woman chased after the little boy and pulled him away as Riley passed. Everyone was silent. Only the sound of Riley's bare feet dragging across the hot ground made noise. As she passed the fifth hut, she saw the brunette woman who had been there when she woke up. The familiar face was walking toward her. She was accompanied by a curly-haired man. Both parties stopped a few feet away from each other. Riley stared at them with fear in her eyes.

"Don't worry, Riley," said the man with a calm voice. "All of you, back to work," he commanded to the women of the dusty village. "This is Adelay." He gestured to the brunette woman with his hand. "She has been watching you for the past three days."

"Wait. What?" asked Riley, confused.

"You have been sleeping for three moon cycles," said Adelay in a dreamy voice.

"By that, we mean that you have been unconscious for quite some time. Adelay has been giving you hourly sedatives made from the herbs grown from our gardens to help you get well," the man reassured her. "My name is Zahid," he said, holding out a rough, hairy hand which Riley shook cautiously.

"I was sick?" she asked. Riley looked from Adelay to Zahid for confirmation.

"You seemed troubled, and I wouldn't blame you. You have seen what most men have not." He looked at her softly, and she could see a smile forming beneath his beard. "We did expect this when we accepted to take you in." Zahid moved out of the way and gestured for her to walk with him along the dirt road. Adelay made her way back to the hospital hut.

"What do you mean?" she asked.

"Your troubles with the shadow creatures," he said.

"Well you could have saved a lot of time and gas just by having Tooth and Stone ask me whether I even needed your help," she said irritated.

"Fang and Rocky," he corrected with a chuckle. "But you do need our help."

"No offence, but you don't seem like you're in the position to be protecting someone," she said. "And no, actually, your help isn't needed. The shadow creature has been killed." With a wave of his hand, Zahid made clear that he did not wish for Riley to continue speaking.

"Firstly," he said in a slightly more serious tone, "please don't let our conditions fool you. We are well prepared and trusted for your protection." He smiled at her, and they continued their walk. "But I believe you are the one who is mistaken; I'm speaking of all shadow creatures – not simply the two that were managed to be killed."

Riley stopped and looked at him as he drew closer to a group of mud huts at the end of the dirt road. "What?" she said anxiously. "Two?" she repeated.

Zahid looked quizzical about the worried expression on Riley's face. "Of course, one was at the park in the city of Georgia and the other in your own home. Certainly you'd know that. Fang told me you were present for both encounters."

"Fang?" she asked, drawing closer. "Since when was he there?"

"Well, since Monsignor of the Fallsdale church contacted me on the day you came to him. He said the Devil sent his demons after you. Naturally, I sent Fang and Rocky to immediately watch over you," he explained while resting a large, hairy hand on her shoulder.

"Then why didn't they help when I was trying to save my brother?" she hissed.

"Fang is still quite young, as you may have noticed, and our dear Rocky has lost his touch," he said lamentably. "They tried to stay out of sight, and they missed your encounter with the shadow creature that murdered your dear stepbrother. For that, I apologize." He looked down at Riley's disturbed eyes and smiled sweetly. "They did, however, travel uphill to where they found the shadow creature dying. I don't understand how, Riley. You've made a really powerful friend – a shadow figure. He had much to do with this defeat, I imagine?"

"I don't understand," she said, looking at Zahid anxiously. "I thought there was only one shadow creature – but two?" Riley was still processing the news of there being more than one demon lurking in the forest in Georgia.

"No, I'm afraid you still don't understand. There are as many shadow creatures as there are human beings on this planet." They walked along the path into the center of the group of mud huts. Men entered and exited the huts wearing the same torn clothing as the woman and children.

"That's a lot to kill," she said in a defeated tone. "But I don't get it," she said as Zahid stopped in front of a wooden cabin much like the one she had awoken in. "Where are they coming from?"

"I will explain as much as I know in good time; however, I must leave you for now," he said. He pointed to a young man with short black hair and a red shirt who exited the large wooden cabin. "Fang is to accompany you." Riley rolled her eyes. "Wish me luck," he said to Fang.

"Good luck, sir," Fang said as Zahid left straight away around the cabin.

"Where's he going?" Riley thought out loud.

"Gone to patrol the forests around us with the rest of the village's men," answered Fang.

"Women and children stay behind?" jeered Riley.

"For your information, I have become of age. I volunteered to show you around," said Fang with a glare in his eyes.

"Come of age? You guys are way too formal for..." she ended her thought when she noticed the saddened look in his eyes.

"For living here," he finished in a hushed tone and bowed his head slightly.

Riley felt a ball of pressure rise in the back of her throat. She looked away as a silence came between them, and they watched the men continue to leave toward the dark green forest that enclosed the village. "What is this place?" she asked, breaking the silence. She looked around at the dozen mud huts and then to Fang, who smirked.

"You're in the Valley of Hay," he said with a smile. He began walking, and she followed. "This is the safest place on the planet. I should apologize before we start. I didn't mean to hurt you three moon cycles ago, but you weren't cooperating. It was for your own good."

"Did you really think I'd let you steal me away from my home?" she smirked.

"Of course not, Riley Orel, but we did hope you'd listen. I suppose we were wrong," he said, his tone relaxed and powerful for his size.

"How old are you?" Riley asked.

"I'm nineteen, Riley Orel," he said coolly.

Fang guided her around the group of huts and into a marketing lot. "This is where trading gets done," he said. Women at work were all stationed behind counters beneath gazebos big enough to fit only a single person in each. They walked through the market on a dirt trail which led to another wooden cabin with crosses carved on both sides of the dark wooden door. "The healing stations mark both ends of the village," he said as they came to a stop. "Cultivation is done on both sides of the village, as you can see. One of the agricultural zones is over that way," he pointed at a large field to the left of the hospital. The field was filled with shrubbery and plants sprouting out from the soil. "The other cultivation area is, in the same way, to the left of the healing station back at the other end of the village."

Every man, woman, and child of the Valley of Hay were as dark haired as Riley was fair. She found it quite annoying as well that each person here was as strikingly beautiful as Parker. Eyes continued to follow her as she walked through the market. The delicious smell of the cooked food made her stomach ache. She admired the jewellery and stopped to watch an elderly woman in beige robes sitting on the dirt ground at a knee-high table. Children circled her as she shuffled a deck of playing cards. The old woman smiled at the children as she placed two cards face down on the wooden table. She flipped one, revealing a ten of hearts and smiled at a little boy kneeling in front of her. She flipped the second card to reveal a nine of hearts, which made her laugh with joy, and the kids around her joined in. The woman put the two cards back into the deck and began shuffling once again. She pulled out a card from the deck and placed it face up revealing a queen of hearts. The old woman stared curiously at the card. She picked the card back up and examined it in the sunlight then placed it back onto the table with a worried expression. She shuffled the deck a couple times more, pulled out a second card, and placed it next to the queen. As the ace of spaces was revealed, the woman's piercing eyes shot upward to meet Riley's. Made uncomfortable by the situation, Riley hesitantly stumbled back to Fang.

"Who is that woman?" she asked, pointing at the old card dealer.

"That's Mabel Mildred, the eldest of the village," he said in a hushed tone. "She is the only person permitted to study and practice Wiccan magic."

"Magic!" Riley chuckled while watching Mabel Mildred. "She does know it doesn't exist, right?" She looked back at Fang and noticed his eyes sharpen.

Feeling that she crossed a line, Riley quickly turned away from his deadly gaze and noticed the sunlight shining off a large, metallic one story building across the valley by the edge of the forest. "What's that?" she asked as they drew closer to the end of the dirt road.

"That is off limits," said Fang. He walked up beside her to the front of the hospital cabin. "Only men are allowed to enter it. I am unsure what it is used for, actually. Zahid will soon take me there like he has done for my brothers."

Riley smirked at his comment regarding his age. She looked back at the metallic building. A voice in her head tempted her: *Open it, Riley.*

Riley answered the voice. *If only Fang would leave.*

"It's about time for the midday meal," he said as he examined the sky. "The sun is at its highest." Fang urged Riley back into the group of mud huts where Zahid had left them. He then invited her into the wooden cabin he had emerged from an hour ago.

Riley walked into a small room about the size of her kitchen. A table was surrounded by four dark wooden chairs and light brown walls. Paintings of forests hung on the walls, and a wooden bookshelf sat next to the entrance to another room across from the main door. Fang crossed the hardwood floor into the next room as Riley made her way to the table in the middle.

Riley waited as the sound of a running faucet came from the next room. She was sure she heard the sound of weeping being muffled by the running water. She walked over to the entrance to the other room, which looked like a small kitchen. A large cupboard lined the wall. Fruits and vegetables lay on the counter beside the sink. As Riley entered, a tall, dark, dirty-haired, shirtless man walked into the room, and his eyes fixed on her.

"Another one!" he shouted, and a girlish whimper sounded by Riley's feet.

She looked down to her right at an orange-haired woman, who knelt on the floor, picking up broken plate shards. Tears welled in the woman's eyes. She had nothing but a dirty old cloth to wrap around her body as clothing. Fang entered from behind the shirtless man with a towel in his hands, drying them off.

"Ambro!" said Fang. He looked alarmed at the hairy man. "This is Riley Orel." Fang made his way back to the counter and picked up a plate of finger foods and dip while the man known as Ambro went into the wooden cupboard and pulled out a new plate. He mumbled to himself angrily.

"You know what?" said Ambro to Fang with the plate in hand. "I don't care if you're fond of this one. It's not staying." The young, orange-haired woman quickly glanced upward at Ambro. His grip broke the plate he held. "Not again!" he yelled as he ran toward her. "You are mine!" Ambro grabbed her from the back of the head and pulled her closer to his face. With a smack to the face, the young woman fell back to the floor. "And the same goes for you," said Ambro, pointing at Riley.

"Riley Orel!" yelled Fang into Ambro's face, which froze immediately. "The girl we watch," he whispered.

Riley stood, horrified. She looked pityingly at the orange-haired woman, who wiped her eyes with fingers covered by tiny shards of glass. She continued to clean the mess. Riley glared back at Ambro as she found the voice she had lost moments ago. "How dare you hurt her? You're the one who broke the plate. Maybe if you had controlled your anger, it wouldn't have happened" she hissed. Ambro's nose flared as he looked down at Fang, who stayed glued to the spot he stood in between Ambro and herself.

"Oho, she's got a mouth on her, Fang! Better watch her or she'll end up like Katrina – just another part of Mable's act." Ambro glared back at Riley and purposefully bumped into Fang as he walked out of the room. He slid through the doorway and slammed the front door shut.

Riley knelt to the ground and helped the orange-haired woman clean the plate shards up off the floor.

"Riley," whispered Fang, turning to her, "you don't have to."

"But I'm gonna," she hissed. "He's an ass. Why doesn't anyone help her? Why don't you?" She glared accusingly at Fang.

"It's alright, Miss Orel. I'm fine," the orange-haired woman ensured. "See, I don't hurt long. I am happy to work for him."

"You're not happy," said Riley, but she got no reply. The maid continued to clean the shards off the ground, and Riley kept insisting on helping but was discouraged to do so each time.

Fang lowered himself onto his knees. "If Ambro comes home and sees you helping her, she will be in even bigger trouble. She is supposed to work with no help whatsoever. It is part of her deal." Fang stood up quickly with a blank expression on his face.

Riley stood up and noticed Fang's unblinking eyes and clenched fists. "Her deal?" she asked.

"No," he said shaking his head. "No."

"Come on what is it?" she urged.

"It is none of your business!" snapped the orange-haired girl as she began to clean up the shards from the second plate.

Riley glared at her and followed Fang, who walked into the dining room. "You know what?" she said staring into his worried eyes. "I don't care. Now is that it here? I'd like to go."

"You haven't eaten," he said blankly.

She grabbed a couple of carrots off the platter. "There. Now I want to go home."

"You can't," said Fang, coming back to his senses. "You have to stay until protection is no longer required."

"Fang, it is no longer needed. If you say you're protecting me, then think of how I feel here. My brother just died. If you keep me here, I'll miss his funeral. This isn't my home. This isn't where I'm safest, and this isn't where I want to be." Riley spun around and made her way to the front door as Fang ran up in front of her.

"Where you going?" he asked as he ran up in front of her.

"Home." She pushed him out of her way.

"But you don't know where to go," he said, grabbing hold of her wrist. He released as she took a step backward.

"I'm gonna get out of here and find out where I really am because the Valley of Hay doesn't ring a bell."

"Of course it doesn't – it is the safest place in the world," he interrupted. "This is why you must stay."

"Listen to me!" She pointed a carrot at him. "Where I'm from, no one beats on the help. I honestly feel less safe here than when I was sleeping in the company of Peck." Riley turned and walked out the door. She headed toward the hospital cabin she had woken up in.

"Wait!" called Fang as he ran up to her.

"God, kid – give up! I will not stay here."

"I am not kid," he spat. "I am a man."

"If you were really a man then you wouldn't let your father beat on that woman."

"Brother," he corrected her in a weak tone.

"Same difference." She stormed off leaving Fang on the dirt road.

Upon entering the hospital cabin, Riley found Adelay, her nurse, making up the beds at the back of the room. Adelay smiled at her sweetly and continued her work.

"Where can I find my own clothes?" she asked Adelay once beside her.

Adelay smiled at her and stood up straight at Riley's height. She looked from Riley to the nightgown she wore. "I don't have your clothes with me at this moment, but I do have some extras I don't mind lending." Adelay opened a large cupboard by the door opposite from the entrance and revealed many identical beige outfits – the same clothes each of the men, women, and children of the village wore – everyone besides Fang.

"I'm sorry, Adelay, but I'm leaving for home, so I kind of need my clothes," she explained.

"I am sorry but I cannot do that," she said smiling.

"Do what?" asked Riley worryingly.

"Allow you to leave, of course." Adelay shut the cupboard door behind her. "When you are done changing, you can leave for the gardens and do some chores like the rest of the women." Riley could have sworn she heard regret in Adelay's tone but was too angry to care.

She slipped on the beige shorts and short sleeve shirt after Adelay left the cabin. Riley opened the cabin door slowly, to avoid the gaze of suspecting eyes. She planned to sneak out through the front entrance of the village, but to her misfortune, the nurse had been waiting on the other side of the door to personally escort her to the garden.

Chapter 10

Even the late summer in the Valley of Hay was warmer than what Riley had adapted to in Fallsdale. While her hometown would soon be waking up to a frosty glaze over the grass, here, the soil was as dry as ever. For the next two weeks, Riley was under constant supervision by the village women and was forced to do her work when neither the men nor children were around. Riley occasionally picked fights with those who tried to mistreat her as Ambro had done to the orange-haired servant; however, the women were much stronger than they seemed. Fang kept a distance from her; he was still angry about the tone she had taken with him.

The women glared at Riley as she picked perfectly red tomatoes from the garden on the edge of the forest. The silver building in the distance continued to tempt her as she worked. It was the second Sunday of September. Her neck and nose had been burned from the endless work in the gardens under the hot sun. Her beige clothes had turned dirt brown along with her bare feet and broken nails.

Zahid had not made an appearance since their last encounter when he had left to patrol the forests and had left Riley in Fang's care. She was angry at him for disappearing and scared that she would not get out. She had tried escaping on two occasions. On her first attempt, she had tried running out into the gardens toward the forest. The women had released wolves, which they kept in the garden sheds, to herd her back into the garden limits. Her second escape attempt happened during the night when the moon was at its fullest. Every man and woman had been celebrating by pits of fire in the middle of the village. She was certain she would have a clean getaway, but someone must have been on watch because the wolves were released once again.

On this day, however, Riley was back to garden work. The metallic building looked extremely bright as the hot sun reflected off its roof. The voice in her head tempted her: *Open it*. She gazed at the building longingly when a young woman with bright orange hair knelt beside her and began to pick the perfectly red tomatoes.

"Fang convinced Ambro to have me come and help you," she said from the corner of her mouth as she pretended to examine the tomato she held in her hand.

"They're horrible," said Riley, nodding to the woman that walked around the garden and quickly followed suit in pretending to examine her own tomato.

"Of course they are," she said, looking at Riley through the corner of her eye. "From what I've heard," she whispered, "Zahid is interested in you and so is the Howler Child. These women are jealous. You're treated better than any of them by the men and more importantly by the Alpha male and Fang Howler."

"Uh, alright," said Riley as she dropped her tomato into the basket and grabbed a second one. "I don't really know Zahid, and I pissed Fang off. But what's so special about him anyway? He walks around with regular clothes and we get these crappy cloth bags to wear." Riley tugged on her dirty shirt. "Is it something they get to do after leaving the Valley to stalk people?"

"Orel, you have no idea how much these men can know of you just by looking you in the eye. Unlike you, Fang has the ability to forgive easily," she said earnestly. "He's a Howler – the most important family in the Village. They get special treatment."

Riley glared at her. "I can forgive people," she said unconvincingly.

"Not from what I've heard," said the orange-haired girl, who bit her bottom lip as she turned away and dropped another red tomato in the basket.

"Whatever!" Riley hissed and blushed. "Why is Fang's family treated so well?"

The young woman placed her index finger on her mouth and shook her head. "I can't say." Riley sat back in the drying dirt she had watered not long ago and brushed her bangs back behind her ear. "Well, the basket is full enough, and you're in luck," said the orange-haired woman while nodding at what looked like Fang approaching them in the distance. As he walked along the edge of the garden, she noticed his clothes. He wore jean shorts and a blue T-shirt.

Riley stood up quickly from the ground with her basket in her hands. She walked along the tomato plants to the end of the garden alongside her new companion. As they made their way over to Fang, a dark-haired woman stormed up to them with anger in her eyes.

"What do you think you're doing?" she spat at Riley.

"I'm done," said Riley, handing her the basket full of red tomatoes. She continued to walk by the woman to get to Fang but stopped when she heard the woman giving the orange-haired servant trouble.

"I am only here under Ambro's command," she hissed, pulling away from the woman's grip. "I was sent to assist Miss Orel, and I am due back to my master once finished. Should I tell the Howler family about this? Look, here one comes." She nodded her head at Fang. He was smiling and walking toward Riley. As Riley smiled back, surprised at the fact that she was happy to see him, she heard the orange-haired woman whispering darkly to the supervisor. "I'm just about done here, and I swear, if you cause any trouble I will kill you. You know I can, don't you?"

Riley turned back to the two of them, shocked. "I can't believe you said that," said Riley. The garden supervisor walked away angrily, and Fang drew closer. "They're gonna set the wolves on you."

"The wolves don't scare me," she whispered. As Fang reached them, the orange-haired woman walked away.

"Getting along with Amanda Stenmart?" he asked with a bright white smile.

"Ugh, yeah, I guess – at least, more than last time. Thanks for sending her, actually."

"No problem," he said. "How were these last two weeks?" he smirked, looking at her red nose, dirty hands, and dirt-stained clothes.

The day went by faster without the work in the garden. Riley told Fang about her last two weeks in the Valley of Hay. He found it strange that she had been given more work than intended and that she was not asked to work, but forced to.

"Since you were – in a way – kidnapped, you weren't supposed to be working unless you wanted to," he said earnestly as they walked back to the hospital cabin. Riley was angry at the mention of this. She glared at the women who stood in front of the hospital and stared at her. Fang could tell she needed rest, so after walking her to the cabin, he bid her goodnight. With a fresh nightgown on, Riley fell asleep instantly in the hospital bed.

Riley tossed and turned that night. She could hear echoes telling her to "open it." She dreamt of the silver building. She pictured herself opening its doors and a windy scream escaping them. The screaming continued. A wolf howled at her from inside the building.

Riley abruptly sat up in her bed, but the screaming continued to sound and many voices joined in. *Am I dreaming*? She jumped out of bed, ran over to the dark wooden door, and pulled it open. Men, women and children were scattering from every direction. Riley walked out onto the cold dirt road. The moon and torches were the only sources of light. What sounded like a child's scream continued to sound from inside one of the mud huts. Riley made her way over to the source along with all of the men. She peered over shoulders for a better look and saw a child being dragged out from the hut with a severely wounded leg. Blood stained the young girl's nightgown. The men formed a circle around the girl. Adelay was followed by Mabel Mildred as she entered the circle.

The men surrounding Riley entered the hut, and growls instantly emerged from inside. Riley could hear hissing and tables falling over. Finally, the men emerged with a very small wolf that continued to struggle angrily in their arms.

"My daughter!" screamed a woman as she fought to break free from the men that were holding her by the hut next door. "Please, that's my daughter!" Riley could not take her eyes of the struggling mother.

The circle surrounding commotion broke again, and Riley saw the injured girl as a man quickly carried her into the hospital cabin with Adelay at his side. Mabel Mildred remained in the circle, speaking to what looked like a purple crystal in her hands.

The men holding the wolf had much trouble keeping it in a tight grip; the little wolf yelped and spun around trying to break free. It scratched and bit any arm it could reach until one of the men finally smacked it over the head with his bare hands. The mother of the wounded girl continued to scream and cry as she was held away from her daughter.

Open it. Open the door. The voice returned. Riley surveyed the area: people were laughing with joy, others were crying hysterically. There was great commotion. She could easily get away. She began to casually walk back to her cabin and ducked behind the corner before anyone could notice. She waited for a moment against the wall of the cabin, hoping no one would come. Riley stepped quietly around the edge of the cabin and encouraged herself to make a run for the forest, which was brightly lit by the moon and stars in the sky. She edged the wall cautiously and abruptly stopped in her footsteps when she saw a large grey wolf sniffing around the field she was about to make a break for. The wolf's nose led it closer, and it gained speed as it drew near to Riley. She began to breathe unsteadily. The wolf's head lifted from the ground and growled at Riley as she made a run for the forest.

A howl erupted from behind her, and many unseen wolves howled back. Riley kept running, but before she knew it, something smacked her in the head. Her body fell limp onto the cold, wet ground, and everything went black.

The right side of Riley's face prickled. She felt herself waking but could not open her eyes. She could feel a hand massaging her bruise, easing the pain. The hand eventually pulled away. Riley opened her eyes to see Adelay by her beside once again.

"You were unconscious when we found you," said Adelay dreamily as she put medicine bottles back in a rolling cart at the end of the bed. "Can you tell me what happened?"

"I don't know. I can't remember," stammered Riley while touching her tender face. "Something hit me," she said. In Adelay's cart, Riley found a mirror to inspect her bruising, but there were no marks on her face. She touched her cheekbone, and to her surprise, it did not hurt. She placed the glass mirror back on Adelay's cart lightly and slipped back to the head of her bed where she sat, puzzled.

Adelay smiled and turned away with her rolling medicine cart. She placed the cart in the corner of the room before leaving the hut. Feeling more conscious, Riley surveyed the rest of the room, and was surprised to find Zahid sitting at the other side of her bed.

"Fang has told me you don't like it here too much," he said placidly.

"Not really," she said, grimacing while sliding out of bed. "I haven't seen you in a while."

"I have been training Fang," he chuckled. "But that's not important; I just wanted to make certain that you were not harmed during last night's activities."

"Yeah, what was all that about with the little girl?" she asked hastily, looking around the room for the child who she had seen being carried into this very cabin.

"She is fine," said Zahid in his calm tone, smiling through his black beard. "She was returned to her family this morning."

"And the wolf?"

"It has been taken care of. Now I must be off. I will be seeing you very soon, and I apologize for my absence. I have been busy."

"Yeah, ok," she said as he left the cabin.

Riley changed into her dirt-stained clothes and followed suit. She walked down the dirt road while the women watched her angrily. Their pet wolves growled as she passed by. She spotted Fang walking around a group of mud huts at the end of the road. Today, both Fang and Zahid were wearing the same beige outfits as everyone else. As Fang spotted Riley, a smile formed across his face.

"Hmm," she smirked. "Decided to blend in with everyone else today?"

"It is much more comfortable in the jeans, but tomorrow is my first day in the forest so I thought I would give it a try," he said happily.

The voice in her head beckoned: *Open the bright door.* She shook the voice out of her head and tried to focus on the present. "So, Zahid has been training you?"

"Yes," he hesitated.

"So he brought you into the building?" she smiled, trying to sound as casual as possible.

"It was my time, yes," he answered, still seeming unsure about the proper way to respond.

"So uh, what's in it?"

Fang's eyes sharpened. "I'm not to tell anyone, Riley Orel," he said as calmly as he could.

"Fine, sorry," she said. "I'm just curious. I thought I'd be allowed to know because I'm not really one of the women from around here," she mumbled to herself in a voice just loud enough for Fang to hear.

The rest of their day together went by decently quick. Riley occasionally brought up the shining building but always ended in mid sentence when she would notice Fang's glares. They walked along the gardens as the workers glared at her as well; Riley ignored them.

"You guys have pet wolves," she stated later that evening while Fang walked her back to the hospital cabin.

"Yes we do."

"But isn't that uh…"

"Dangerous?" Fang completed her sentence.

"Yeah," she whispered.

"Wolves aren't dangerous, Riley Orel," he assured her. "But if you anger them, they may bite."

"I thought they killed people?" she said tentatively while watching Fang shake his head.

"It is very rare for a wolf to harm a human being for no reason," he said placidly.

"But that little girl?" she asked, recalling the previous night.

"That was an accident," he said as they stood in front of the dark wooden door of the hospital cabin.

Fang smiled at her with his straight, white teeth and wished her goodnight before he left for his own wooden cabin. Riley walked through the dark wooden door and to her surprise, found a dark-haired little girl lying in the first bed beside the wall. She was sleeping silently on her back. For a moment, Riley thought that this was the girl from the wolf attack, but as she looked closer, this girl seemed much older. Her hair was about a foot longer, and it rested in pigtails on both sides of her head.

On the far side of the room, Riley grabbed the perfectly folded nightgown off her bed and changed clothes in the shadows. Finally resting in her bed, she let herself fall into another deep sleep.

Chapter 11

◊ ◊ ◊

Riley ran deeper into the forest. Her blonde hair flew in her face, and her arms swung at full speed. She was running around frantically looking for something. "Where are you?" she heard herself call out. Her voice grew evermore distant until she could barely hear anything. She ran faster as the ground began to tremble. She turned and saw the wolves chasing her. Something big and dark ran alongside them. As madly as she swung her arms and legs, they could not run any faster. She was panting and on the verge of giving up. The hairy hands closed in on her, and she was held tight against the beast's breast. "No you have to help!" she screamed. Her screaming was muffled until she could not hear herself anymore and sat up, shocked, in the cabin bed.

She breathed heavily as she looked around the room. The little girl had already left or had been taken away. Adelay suddenly came stomping in through the front door, her white nightgown trailing on the ground. Tears flowed from her eyes as she passed by directly into her room without any word. Riley stared at the door Adelay had entered, completely surprised by the nurse's erratic behaviour. She slid out of bed and pressed her ear quietly to Adelay's door.

No sound came from behind the door; there was no sobbing or

creaking floor boards – just complete silence. As Riley pulled her ear away to knock, Adelay wrenched the door wide. She swung a beige cloth bag over her shoulder and marched into the main room where Riley slept. She had only been inside her private quarters for a minute, however, her skin and hair now looked like she had gone to a spa. She was wearing dark jeans and a tight, purple long-sleeved shirt. Adelay's quick change of appearance stunned Riley for a moment.

"Adelay?" said Riley dumfounded.

"Yes, Riley," said Adelay in a tone of complete control. "I know I'm very fast." As she turned to leave, Riley suddenly found her voice.

"What are you doing?" she asked, confused.

"Something you can't," she snapped. "I'm getting out of here." She turned and began to walk back to the door as she muttered to herself. "They're not getting me," she said and slammed the door shut.

Riley ran after Adelay. She flung the door open but could not see any sign of her. As she ran around the cabin, three dark haired women glared at her as they walked the perimeter of the village. Riley walked back into the cabin to throw on her dirt stained clothes, wondering how Adelay was able to get away so quickly and without anyone noticing.

Riley walked along the dirt road toward the group of mud huts, hoping to find Fang. As she searched, a woman, who Riley recognized as the guard Amanda Stenmart had snapped at in the garden, approached her with a sneer on her face.

Riley tried to avoid the tall, dark-haired woman, but she stepped in front of the path, blocking Riley's way. "What do you want?" Riley hissed.

"I just wanted to let you know," said the woman in a threatening voice, "that when neither the Howler nor the Alpha male are around, you'll have something waiting for you." The woman raised her fist and cracked her knuckles in Riley's face.

"You look really stupid," Riley confessed easily. "You do know that right?"

The woman towered over Riley, who shoved her aside as she continued on her way to Fang's wooden cabin. She walked hastily on the hot dirt road with bare feet. She brushed her wet bangs out of her face as she drew near to his cabin. Upon arriving at the familiar cabin, she knocked three times before letting herself in.

"Good morning," said Fang happily while walking into the room with a plate full of cinnamon buns. "Are you hungry? Plans have changed – I am not patrolling until noon, so I can stick around."

"Good," Riley said. "I've at least got my morning to sit around, but later when you go, I'll have no choice but to work in the gardens," she said, sulking into the chair nearest the front entrance.

They sat at the dining table while they ate the icing-covered cinnamon buns. Riley peered through the open doorway across from the table, looking for Amanda Stenmart. It seemed the orange-haired servant was not in the kitchen.

"Where's Amanda?" she asked as she swallowed a mouthful of her cinnamon bun.

"Amanda? Oh, she's just getting firewood" said Fang, pausing to turn and peer into the kitchen.

Riley nodded while she grabbed a second bun. She questioned whether to let Fang know about Adelay running away.

"So… Everything okay lately?" he asked, reaching for another bun.

"Yeah, I guess." Fang watched her closely as she fiddled with the sticky food in her hands. "Well I mean, Adelay was a little angry this morning," she said.

At these words, Fang shot up straight in his seat and paid close attention to what Riley said. "She was what?" he asked with complete seriousness.

"She was a little angry, and she stormed out of the cabin," Riley answered, confused about the importance of the situation.

Fang did not have a chance to respond as Ambro came stumbling forcefully into the room. Amanda Stenmart followed behind, her face covered in sweat and dirt.

"Ambro!" called out Fang, jumping to his feet. "Vandarg is showing unaccepted emotions."

Ambro's eyes widened as a crooked smile ran across Amanda Stenmart's face.

"That's impossible," said Ambro, scratching the top of his balding head. "The elixir…"

"Yes, exactly. What if she was lying?" asked Fang. "What if it was not everlasting? If the elixir was functional, Adelay would not know of her abilities. She would not know what she is. She would not be showing signs of disobedience."

Both Ambro and Fang immediately ran out the front door, leaving Amanda Stenmart and Riley in the cabin. Riley looked from the open door back to the orange-haired woman, puzzled. Amanda on the other hand smiled and took a seat at the table across from Riley.

"What was that about?" asked Riley, pointing to the opened door with her thumb.

"No idea," said Amanda, coolly.

Amanda grabbed a bun from Fang's plate and ate while Riley watched her uncertainly. Fang had been gone for some time while Amanda finished the breakfast he had made. She smiled at Riley and kept directing her attention to the open door as though waiting for something. Sure enough, a large, dark-haired, and sturdily-built man came up into the cabin and glared at her after nodding politely to Riley.

"Stenmart," he commanded vigorously in a deep voice.

Amanda winked at Riley as she stood up from her chair without any fuss and walked by the tall, tanned man. The man smiled at

Riley before leaving with Amanda at his side. Riley abruptly stood from her chair and hurried to Amanda's side, looking anxious.

"What's going on?" asked Riley, keeping up with their quick pace.

"Something horrible for them, I can tell you that much," said Amanda, gleaming with delight.

"Hey!" shouted the man following Amanda. He stopped and stepped in front of Amanda, making her bump into him. He towered over her angrily without blinking. "Don't forget your orders," he whispered, breathing deeply on her face.

Amanda smiled as though in complete control. She nudged the towering man over as she continued walking toward the market. In the center of the market, a large pile of firewood had been neatly stacked and was circled by a black powder on the ground. As the three of them drew closer to the wood pile, Zahid appeared from behind the second hospital cabin alongside Fang, Ambro, and a dark-haired man. The unfamiliar man had grey eyes and a darker tan than Fang. He was slightly shorter than Ambro. Zahid and the three men met them by the firewood, looking outraged at Amanda. Fang was the only one who did not wear an expression of disgust or hatred for her. Instead, his expression was filled with sorrow, and he looked away from her every few moments.

"You knew," hissed Zahid.

Amanda smirked and gave a light chuckle. "What are you talking about, Zahid?"

Zahid's beard twitched and, to Riley's amazement, his eyes darkened. Zahid rubbed his eyes, and he looked as though he would love nothing more than to hurt Amanda. "The elixir!" he yelled, grasping his fists at the air with uncontrolled fury. "You knew," he whispered darkly. His eyes flickered to Riley. He then took a step back while turning a light shade of red. "Fang," he commanded. Fang quickly approached Riley to pull her away, but she kept her place.

"Zahid," said Amanda, still smirking. "I was too young to ever understand any of that crap." She winked at Riley while the young man Riley did not recognize took a step closer, glaring. Zahid huffed and looked away from Riley's eyes while Fang still struggled to remove her from the situation. Zahid, filled with rage, quickly turned to Amanda and smacked her across the face before leaving the hospital cabin followed by Ambro and the younger man. They headed toward the silver building.

Amanda smiled and brushed her fingers lightly over Riley's hair and shoulders. She turned to Fang, who glared at her, and she winked before walking back toward the group of mud huts. Riley was struck silent for a moment. She turned to Fang with questions burning in her mind, but Fang just shook his head and walked off after Zahid.

Riley had no clue as to what anyone was talking about. She stood, barefoot, on the warming dusty road. Down the path, she noticed Mabel Mildred, who was sitting in the exact place where Riley had first come across her. The old grey-haired woman shuffled her playing cards as she stared at Riley. She glared as she pulled out a card from its deck and examined it. Riley looked away and noticed the tall dark-haired woman she had encountered earlier that morning. The woman remained next to a jewellery counter and sneered at Riley. She decided it might be safest to find Amanda for answers to all her questions.

She walked back toward Fang's cabin, feeling the women's eyes watching her every step. The tension grew stronger as the cabin drew nearer; every tall and beautiful woman Riley passed paused to watch her. She restrained herself from looking at them. She maintained as much of an impassive expression as she could. Riley watched through her peripherals, and the women did not seem convinced. They continued to sneer as she walked swiftly into Fang's cabin, slamming the door shut.

Riley gasped as she noticed Amanda, who was standing on a dark wooden chair that was pushed up against the wall. Amanda held a large knife that she was forcefully jabbing into the wooden wall. She stuck the blade into the wall and dragged it downward. Amanda looked back at Riley and smiled before she jumped off the chair and directed her attention back to the wall she had just ruined. She had carved the word "CURSED" into the wall of Fang's cabin. Amanda nodded approvingly and turned back to Riley with the dark wooden chair in her hands to place it back underneath the table. Riley stared wide-eyed at the marked-up wall while Amanda giggled and grabbed the dirty plate she had eaten from earlier that morning and brought it into the kitchen.

Amanda returned, beaming with delight. Riley still could not believe her eyes. "They're gonna kill you," said Riley, prying her eyes away from the wall. Amanda just chuckled and took a seat at the wooden table. "Amanda, what are you doing?" she asked as she brushed her fingers over the carved word.

"Screwing with Ambro," she answered. "Fang's alright though," she admitted.

Riley leaned against the wall and drew a breath before speaking. "Whatever, I don't care," she said truthfully and brushed her bangs back behind her ear. "But what I don't understand is what all that drama earlier was about." She pointed a dirt covered finger toward the door.

Amanda smiled and nodded slightly.

"Like, why were they angry at you?" Riley added, feeling annoyed that the Valley of Hay brought more questions than answers.

"Oh, it's nothing," she said, waving a hand between them.

"Yes, it's something," shot Riley.

"Look," said Amanda with a smile, "we're having a bonfire tonight—"

"I don't care about your stupid bonfire!" Riley interrupted.

"Really?" she asked, making an obviously fake confused

expression. "Aside from Adelay, you're the first person I've met who has hated the Valley of Hay bonfires."

Riley's expression went blank. *What is she talking about? Why won't she tell me what's going on?* Riley shook her head and took a seat next to Amanda, who kept smiling at Riley's confusion.

"Well anyway," continued Amanda after a short silence, "when you're put to bed tonight along with the rest of those children, you should sneak over to the fire and check things out."

Riley watched her tentatively from her seat. As Ambro's slave, she would not be able to speak of things he had unauthorized her to speak of. Amanda sat back in her chair while Riley pondered about the upcoming night and how she would try to find a way to the market where perhaps something was to happen.

"Alright," said Riley finally. "I think I'll do that."

Amanda still smiled in her seat as she wiped off her knife and placed it back down on the table in front of her.

◊ ◊ ◊

As time crept by, Riley tried finding things to do on her own. Fang had not returned; he was most likely on his first forest patrol. She walked back and forth through the village from one hospital cabin to the next, trying to avoid the angry woman who threatened her earlier that day.

She made a stop at Fang's cabin one last time, looking for answers or just company. Feeling hungry, she made her way to the kitchen for a snack. It was there that she found Amanda completely surrounded by food. She was sitting at the counter eating everything she could find and throwing the garbage on the floor. Riley watched, speechless again at Amanda's daring behaviour. "Don't forget to check out the fire tonight," Amanda said as she left the cabin through the back door.

Riley searched the kitchen for something Amanda had left over to eat. After finding an apple hidden on top of the refrigerator, Riley left the cabin and headed down the dirt road. A man bumped into her on the path and gave her orders to get to bed. She walked back to the hospital cabin with her apple in hand and watched the village children run into their mud huts as if on cue. The village men came out of their huts and all casually headed toward the market.

In her hospital cabin, Riley undressed and threw on her nightgown as she prepared for bed. She kept directing her attention to both doors of the cabin. It was strange that she had not seen Adelay at all since she stormed out earlier that morning. She wondered if Adelay had managed to successfully escape and wished Adelay would have taken her along.

Riley jumped into bed and waited for what seemed like a long time but probably was not. A man poked his head through the front door to check on her and left in a hurry. As soon as he had gone, Riley jumped out of bed and ran over to the door. She listened carefully for any guards or wolves before opening the door just a crack to make sure she was safe.

She stepped out cautiously, shutting the door gently and looked around for any guards or wanderers. She walked along the dirt road, inches away from the group of mud huts in the market. A rush of adrenaline came over her. *This is it – I'm going for it!* She ran quickly behind the group of huts and ducked behind Fang's cabin. Too afraid to look around the corner, she relied on her hearing to keep her safe from the men in the village. Riley tried not to think about what would happen if she was caught. To her horror, footsteps were heard from the side of the cabin opposite from her. She cupped her mouth with her hand, trying to muffle the sound of her heavy breathing. A wolf ran by the cabin without noticing she was there. The guards were out.

The back of the village was silent. She pulled herself away from the cabin and made her way into the market where laughter erupted, and people began to shout with anger. Riley hid behind a mud hut and peered around the corner. A group of people were watching Mabel Mildred light the bonfire. Zahid was speaking seriously to Fang, Ambro, and the nameless man who Riley had seen earlier that day. Mabel Mildred began to circle the fire, dropping more black powder around it as she walked. When Mabel finished, she lifted her hands into the air and spoke in a language Riley could not recognize. Mabel retreated into the hospital cabin behind the fire and quickly returned with Amanda Stenmart in hand. Riley gasped. *Is this what Amanda wanted me to see? Did she need me to help her?* Riley's heart raced, and she began to panic. Amanda's orange, curly hair hung at her sides, and she brushed it behind her ears as she smiled. She wore only a trace amount of brown cloth around her chest and waist. The villagers yelled angrily.

Riley did not understand what was happening; Amanda was stepping into the small flames, and no one was stopping her. The people were shouting at her to burn faster. Riley's mouth dropped an inch, and she stepped out from behind the mud hut, her nightgown trailing at her ankles.

Amanda knew she was there. Their eyes locked as Amanda smiled at Riley before stepping uncomfortably further into the center of the pile of wood. The flames drew closer. All at once, Fang's eyes followed Amanda's and turned on Riley. His eyes widened and jaw dropped wide. He was petrified and did not move until the nameless man tapped him on the shoulder and looked up at her. The man's eyes sharpened. He turned around to alert Zahid, and the three men watched Riley look with horror at the sight of Amanda as she struggled to stay away from the growing flames.

Zahid sprinted toward Riley as she quickly snapped out of her trance and ran toward the fire to save Amanda. She leapt toward the flames, but something stopped her. She tried forcing herself into the growing fire, but an invisible wall around it prevented her from reaching Amanda.

"Amanda!" she screamed and continually smacked her fists against the invisible wall. Her hands began to bruise and her fingernails bent backward from clawing at the invisible force.

Amanda shook her head. Riley could have sworn she had seen a tear slide across Amanda's cheek, but it had instantly disappeared in the blazing heat. "You can't get in," said Amanda calmly. "The ashes won't let you," she added while pointing to the circle of black powder on the ground that ran the perimeter of the fire.

Riley kept clawing at the invisible wall while a small group of men and women tried to drag her away from the fire. With eyes fixed on Amanda, she continued to struggle against them. Amanda's clothes began to burn. The skin around her legs bubbled as the flames reached her. The orange-haired girl smiled at Riley with tears streaming from her eyes and collapsed into the flames.

"NO!" screamed Riley, fighting off the men and women who held her. "You killed her! You killed her! Murderers!" Riley pointed at Mabel Mildred, who was smiling at Amanda's demise. "I'll kill you!" she screamed. The old woman's smile vanished completely from her face. At the threat of death, she began to shake and ran off without any words.

As Riley raged at the people around her, she began to run out of energy. As everyone's grip on her loosened, Riley sank to her knees and stared at the fire. A large ball swelled back up in Riley's throat. Her breathing turned shallow as if she had given up and did not have the energy to continue letting air in and out of her lungs. Her bangs fell into her face as she sat frozen on the cold dirt ground.

She could see the crowd pulling themselves away as two other men came closer. She figured it was Fang and Zahid but did not care to look at them.

Chapter 12

◊ ◊ ◊

"Zahid! Zahid! She's out of her cabin!" Riley picked herself up enough to see a woman running through the market yelling for Zahid. "Zahid! The Orel girl is out of—" she yelled but stopped in mid sentence when she noticed that her target was kneeling next to a livid Riley.

Zahid stood up and signed the rest of the market crowd away. Without a word, each man and woman turned to head back to their own huts; only Fang remained. Zahid knelt again to lean in closer to Riley. He brought his head close to whisper into her ear, but before he could speak, Riley threw herself on top of him and began to slam her already bruised fists in his face. With one arm, Zahid pushed her off and wiped his bleeding lip while Fang held Riley still. She tossed and pulled while Fang kept her hands gripped behind her back, but as Zahid slapped her across the face, Fang loosened his grip in shock. Riley pulled away and made a run for the forest, but Zahid was faster. He grabbed her by her dirt-stained nightgown, pulled her back, and brushed his dishevelled hair out of his face, feeling slightly embarrassed.

"Riley," he said in a weary voice. "I apologize for that. I must explain."

"Yeah," said Riley nodding her head vigorously. "Yeah you really do have to, and you better have a pretty amazing explanation for all of this because you're all just a bunch of murderers!"

Zahid breathed slowly as Fang came up to his side. "You are in danger," he said calmly. "The Devil has sent his monsters from the shadow world after you." He paused while looking into the burning fire. "This woman here that you've known as Amanda Stenmart was also his worker." He looked weakly into her eyes and put a comforting hand on her shoulder. "We were built for this, all of us here, for protection." Riley gave a puzzled expression. "You are not from here. You have forgotten, Riley Orel," he said staring at her confused expression.

"Forgotten what?" she asked.

Zahid sighed. "Tomorrow, when the sun begins to set, Fang will bring you into the forest with us and—"

"No!" interrupted Riley, remembering her nightmares of the forest beast. Suddenly, everything made sense to her. She would go into the forest with Fang, and that is when the beast would try to take her. She would run until she got tired. It would grab her. She would need to find Fang and help him because it would be Fang she would need to protect.

"What is it Riley?" asked Zahid. He looked shocked at her response.

"I thought you'd be happy that you'll finally get to go into that forest. You've been trying to make it out there so often!" Fang chuckled.

"I was never planning on going in deep," she said with a blank expression, still in deep thought about the beast that would attack her.

"Well, now you will," said Fang hesitantly while looking from Zahid to Riley.

"No." she said flatly. "There is a monster in that forest. If we go in there, it will grab me, and it will hurt you." She pointed at Fang. "Trust me. I have seen it happen. Enough people have been killed here already. We can't go in the forest."

"What are you talking about?" asked Fang.

Zahid looked at Riley with wide eyes, shocked at both the serious tone she was taking and at the prophecy she was telling. He turned quickly as Mabel Mildred came back out from around the corner of the hospital cabin. "You!" he shot angrily at the old woman as he got up and angrily headed toward the fire. He looked to Fang and back to Riley before fixing his eyes on Mabel. "You were wrong!"

"What is it, sir?" asked Fang.

As Riley glared at Mabel, her look of hatred turned into one of horror as the woman hopped into the circle of dark powder and cautiously grabbed handfuls of Amanda's ashes from the center of the pit.

Without warning, Zahid grabbed the scruff of Riley's shirt, distracting her from Mabel's actions. "The Devil is not sending anything after her!" he hissed looking into Riley's blue eyes. "He sent for her. Poor Monsignor was fooled," he added to himself. "Well if it's you he wants, then it's you he'll get," he added in a dark whisper.

Riley looked to Fang, who also seemed unsure of what was happening, and back into Zahid's dark eyes. "Zahid," she pleaded in a quivering voice. "What are you talking about? Are you talking about me?"

Zahid grabbed Riley by the hair and began to forcefully pull her toward the hospital cabin. He made a quick turn around the side of the cabin, tugging tightly on the hair he gripped in his hand. Riley gasped and cried as Fang chased after them.

"Sir!" Fang called as Riley fought to keep her hair from being pulled out. "Sir," Fang repeated breathlessly as he ran to Zahid's side.

"Fang, she was sent here to murder us and save her master. From her own mouth, she said she has seen it happen."

"I was kidnapped by you guys and brought here! I wasn't sent here by anyone but yourselves!" she cried through clenched teeth.

"You knew that Monsignor would send you here if he thought the shadow creatures were after you! You lied to him in order to find an easy route here, didn't you?" Zahid shouted.

"But, sir," said Fang, trying to keep a calm tone with Zahid. "Is it not possible that she has seen a shadow creature in the forest from the village?"

"No." he replied simply. Fang opened his mouth to retort, but Zahid continued with an explanation. "*You* will be hurt and she will be taken away. Those are the words she spoke."

Without a response, Fang followed as Zahid swung Riley forward and began to walk fast toward the silver building. As they finally made their way to the door, Fang watched Riley struggle to keep her balance as Zahid held her off the ground by her hair. Zahid's free hand closed in on the door handle of the metallic building that she had wanted to visit for so long.

Zahid entered and threw Riley forward. She landed on the cold and grey cement floor. Faint lights overhead lit the long hallway. Iron bars lined the walls throughout the hall. Behind each set of bars were cement rooms without any windows. Zahid pulled Riley up from the ground by the scruff of her nightgown and pushed her forward. Riley saw glimmering eyes in the shadows behind large wooden crates and realized that they belonged to wolves that wandered the prison-like building. Zahid shoved her forward every few seconds when she would slow down. Finally, they reached the end of the cold hallway where a large metallic door stood alone in the center of the wall.

Two women approached them and secured Riley's hands behind her back while Zahid went to open the door. She tried to look for a way to escape. She pulled from the women, but their grips were too strong. Her eyes darted everywhere, and they finally landed on the wall to her right. A glass door led to a comfortable room with brown sofas, carpeted flooring, and a light wooden desk. *In the secret hideaway, forever they've kept them. Seek out their devil, and protect him.* The familiar voice in her head began to chant.

I understand, Riley answered back. At the center of this building, Riley realized that the Valley of Hay must be the "secret hideaway," and whatever was behind the metallic door Zahid was currently unlocking, would be their devil.

The door swung open and revealed a dark cement cell. Opposite from the door was a small barred window which let in a bit of light from the beautiful starry sky. Zahid grabbed Riley from the two women and threw her into the shadows. "Go to your master," he said. The door slammed shut, and a clicking sound was heard from the outside as he locked it back up. On all fours, Riley squinted and looked frantically around the small, dark cell for some sign of the terror which she was surely about to encounter. Knives and building tools hung on the cement wall to the right, and cracks and slashes marked the wall to the left. She stood up off the cold ground and looked into the dark corner by the marked wall. Something was breathing heavily in the shadows.

Riley stepped backward toward the metallic door as rustling noises came from the dark corner. As her muscles tightened against the far wall, a pale hand emerged from the shadows. The hand rested on the cement floor in the small patch of light let in by the window. Riley braced herself, covering her head with her arms.

"White Witch?" asked a weak and boyish voice.

Riley peered through the cracks between her fingers. Her breathing shook as a second hand appeared in the starlight. The hand was followed by a lolling head with long, dark hair. The hidden face looked up from the ground to Riley, revealing a weak boy with beautiful, brown eyes and a greasy face. On all fours, the young boy crawled out from his corner and lay at Riley's feet.

"He said you'd come, White Witch. He told me you would," said the boy. He looked up at her face. The boy stumbled up onto his feet, standing two inches shorter than Riley. He gazed softly into her blue eyes.

"Umm," said Riley, trying to make sense of everything she was hearing. "You're the—"

"Devil," interrupted the young boy. He immediately dropped his face into his hands, sank back into his dark corner, and began to sob. "No," he whimpered from within the darkness. "He told me you wouldn't understand."

"Who told you?" she asked, dropping to her knees.

The boy's face emerged from the dark corner, and his mouth opened to answer, but he bit down on the words to think. "The man in my head."

Riley's heart jerked. She felt goose bumps form all along the back of her neck. She watched him as he slipped back into the dark corner. His outline was still visible as her eyes adjusted to the darkness.

"White Witch, I'm begging you," he dropped onto his knees into the moonlight, looking weaker than ever, and swayed as he spoke. "Please don't make me fight with you."

"What are you talking about?" asked Riley, taking a few steps back. "I don't understand."

"You have to save me," he said as tears slid down his cheeks.

"Alright." She knelt down in front of the pitiful boy. Holding his head up in her hands, she looked into his soft eyes. "I'll get you out of here. I promise." She looked at the iron bars and back into his weak gaze as his head shook vigorously.

The boy began to breathe heavily as he reached for Riley's head to copy her motions. He stared into her blue eyes and gave a weak smile that quickly vanished. He began to tremble.

Riley thought there was no way that this boy could be the Devil. He was far too gentle and terrified. "Why?" she asked, pulling away to sit next to him. She looked at the solid door before them and began to pant before continuing. "Why are you in here?"

"Because they think I'm the Devil," he answered.

She looked at his pale, sunken face. He looked like a poor child who had never been taken proper care of. "So there's a man in your head that speaks to you too? Does he like, tell you things in whispers?"

She could see the outline of his head nodding. A great pressure lifted from her. She had finally found someone else that could understand the way she felt. "And the dreams?" she added quickly, startling the boy in the corner. "Tell me everything you know about them." Her high spirits quickly plummeted as the boy stared at her with a confused look. She shook her head at him. "No," she said. "You have to understand. You have the dreams too, don't you?"

"Have to understand what?"

"You have to know what I'm talking about. None of this makes sense unless you know what I'm going through." She kneeled in front of him, anxiously.

"I do dream. Well... I have nightmares." The boy looked away, clearly embarrassed. Riley drew a breath of relief. "I dream about the night I was taken from my parents. I dream about the night they were killed." The boy looked absolutely dreadful.

"Killed?" she repeated.

"Yeah," he answered wearily.

"How long have you been here?" she asked, feeling horrible for the boy. He seemed to be counting in his head. His lips quivered, and he looked her straight in the eyes.

"Since I was two-years-old." He avoided her gaze and stared at the metallic door.

She took in a deep breath and averted her eyes in an attempt to make him feel comfortable. "How long is that?"

"Twelve years," he whispered.

Riley turned to him. Each breath she took burned with rage. She could feel the anger spreading throughout her veins, and she wanted nothing more than to shove Zahid, Mabel, and all of those behind this abuse into the circle of flames to meet their ultimate demise. A fire ignited in her stomach. Riley jumped to her feet and grabbed hold of the axe on the wall. She swung it quickly off its hook, making the knives which hung beside it fall to the cement floor. Riley ran to the door and began to swing the axe over and over again. All of her force was thrown into every swing, but something was not right. The axe left no marks on the door. She threw the axe into a corner and grabbed the first of many saws which hung on the wall. She ran toward the barred window but was blocked from even attempting to saw through the bars by a force similar to the one which prevented her from saving Amanda.

Riley screamed in anger and dropped the saw to the ground. She fell onto her knees, trying to catch her breath. She looked at the wall that was covered with gashes and quickly felt around in the dark for a knife. After finding one on the floor, she slashed at the wall below the window. The knife dug fairly easily into the cement wall. "Could this work?" she asked. After minutes of scraping at the wall, many gashes were visible upon the smooth surface.

The little boy made a noise that sounded like a laugh at her attempts to break free. She turned to him with sweat trickling down her forehead. "They've thought of everything," he said wearily. "They left this equipment in here just to drive me crazy and give me a way to kill myself."

Riley ran her hands over the marks she had made in the wall. She grabbed the knife and furiously aimed her carving into the deepest gash she could find. No matter how hard she pushed, the knife would not go any deeper; it would break the surface but would immediately stop millimetres beneath it.

"It can't go any further," said the boy, shaking his head weakly. He stopped as his eyes began to droop, and he rested his head up against the wall at which Riley kept beating.

She was not going to give up, but the boy was right; she could not cut deeper into the wall. Now covered in sweat, she wiped her forehead and sunk into a sitting position, trying to catch her breath. Riley looked out of the barred window at the starry sky. The thought of being stuck in the Valley of Hay for twelve years continued to make her mind spin with grief. *Will I be able to get out? Will I be able to convince Zahid that what he believes is wrong? Will we be stuck in here forever? What can I do? What can I do?* Anxious and unanswerable questions repeated in her head as she lay sweating on the cold floor and drifted into an uncomfortable sleep.

Chapter 13

A young woman sat on a park bench waiting for her boyfriend to pick her up. She tied her blonde hair into a ponytail with the elastic around her wrist as she sang the song that played on her music player. The phone that was tucked into her jeans began to vibrate. She turned off the music player and put it away before answering her cell. "Hello?" she said, but no one was there. She put the phone back into her pocket and looked at her watch. *Where could he be?* She had been waiting for over an hour for him to arrive. She sat impatiently with her arms and legs crossed. A fly landed on her arm. She smacked it and felt the squish of insect on flesh, but when she removed her hand, it was gone.

Finally, a tall, dark-haired man pulled up in front of her in his beat-up, green car. He was looking over his sunglasses at her with a crooked smile. "Forgive me for being so late, babe," he said as he lightly tapped the passenger seat. A small smile formed across the young woman's face, and she approached the dented car with her traveling bags in hand.

The man's eyes followed her as she hopped into the car and buckled up. He was happy that she was coming with him. He stuck a hand into the pocket of his leather jacket, pulled out a cigarette, and lit it before taking off along the road.

The young woman stared out her window at the city she was leaving behind. She kept waving a fly away with her hand. The bug was annoying her and would not stop buzzing around her head. The man reached an arm around her shoulder as he drove with the cigarette in his other hand. The young woman looked at him and smiled. Something caught her eye; something was gleaming on the back seat. She bent backward a little more to get a closer look at the small cylinder and reached a hand back to grab it while the dark-haired man kept driving. It was a lipstick container. The young woman began to twirl the lipstick in her fingers. She pulled off the lid to reveal a half-used stick of burgundy. She shuddered, and her shouldered tightened underneath his arm. The man turned to see what the problem was. His eyes caught the container of lipstick as the sun glinted off of it, and he froze.

The young woman turned to him, her lips trembling. The man hit the break without warning, and as the car stopped, the fly buzzed around excitedly. She pushed his arm off from around her. He was at a loss for words as he looked at her, begging forgiveness with his eyes. Her eyes, however, were fixed on the lipstick in her lap. Before he could think to say anything, the driver's door flew open. A long, pale green hand reached in and stabbed the man through the chest as the woman screamed and unbuckled herself. She forced the passenger door open, jumped out, and landed with a roll on the ground. She looked around and saw that dozens of hooded creatures with birdlike feet that dangled from beneath their robes were gliding toward the car.

She screamed for help, but no one was around. The man in the car turned pale. The creatures, distracted by young woman's screaming, went after her. After one long, pale green hand pierced her chest, everything went dark.

Riley woke up, huddled in the corner by the wall with the tools. Drenched in sweat, she sat up against the wall and heard a click. She looked over to the door; a second click came from it. Immediately on her feet, Riley hurried to the door, and on the third click, it opened. Her legs instinctively launched forward to find escape, but they were blocked by two large wolves which entered the cell. Their vicious growling sent her back against the wall opposite them.

The man who had been with Ambro and Fang on the previous day walked into the cell and dropped two bowls of porridge onto the floor as Fang came in behind him.

"That's him?" asked Fang, paying no attention to Riley.

"Yeah, pathetic isn't he?" jeered the other man.

The boy sat in his corner trembling as he reached a scrawny hand for one of the bowls.

"So *Hayden*," said the man, stretching out his doubts about the boy's name, "how's it going?" he sneered.

Hayden glared at the man. Fang looked curiously at the boy. For a split second, Riley could have sworn she had seen Fang's eyes quickly dart at her and then back to Hayden.

"He's not the Devil!" cried out Riley.

"Oho!" laughed the other man. "So this is the Nightwatcher? The one who sees the future through dreams?" he said as he walked up to her, his grey eyes staring deep into hers.

"I thought you guys knew," she said weakly.

"Liar!" he yelled. "Smart plan though, I'll give you that, devil-worker." With a raised hand, he silenced the growling wolves. "But the Nightwatcher!" he laughed. "I can't believe it's you!" He looked at Fang, who kept quiet.

The man looked back at her with a grin. "I expected someone stronger… someone who could take out our kind."

"Blake," whispered Fang.

"Yeah I know," he said, turning to Fang. "It's your turn." He turned to the wall full of tools. With a tilted head, he looked to the floor and chuckled when he noticed the knives, axe, and saw. "Make him use whichever one you want." He turned again to Fang. "If you need help, don't be scared to ask." He bumped into Fang's shoulder as he left and shut the door behind him. One wolf stayed behind at Fang's side and sat watching both Hayden and Riley.

Fang walked nervously over to the wall of tools as Hayden whimpered and ate his porridge.

"Fang," said Riley, keeping an eye on the wolf that sat staring at Hayden. "I don't understand what's going on." Fang pulled down a pick axe and examined it thoroughly. "Fang, come on, I trusted you!" she cried, and the wolf growled.

Fang dropped the axe and pulled down a sharp knife. He sighed and stared at her with dark circles around his eyes. "Riley," he said, walking over to Hayden and handing him the knife, "I don't know."

"What are you doing?" she asked as Hayden drew the knife to his own wrist. "Hayden?"

Before she could do anything else, Hayden cut his wrist with the knife and sliced upwards. He pulled the knife away and slammed it onto the cement floor as his voice shuddered. He was panting and holding back tears. Riley ran to him, grabbed the knife, and threw it at the wall opposite from them.

"What are you guys doing to him?" she screamed at Fang, who stepped backward, looking ashamed. The wolf growled.

"Riley," said Fang, but he was interrupted by more shouts from her.

"What the hell, Fang! This is horrible!"

"Riley," he calmly repeated while pointing at Hayden.

With rage in her eyes, she turned to Hayden, who was showing her his wrist which now bore no marks. She quickly grabbed the other one, thinking he was trying to trick her, but no marks were left on either wrist.

"That's why they think I'm the Devil," he said in a weak quivering voice.

She stared at his healed arms, shaking her head. *What is happening? How could any of this be possible? Invisible walls and healing powers?* She backed away on her knees and sat against the wall, bewildered.

Fang stood with his back against the door and his eyes on the knife which Riley had thrown away. The wolf approached him and growled as it shoved him in the ribs with its head. Fang was not moving. He stood transfixed with his mouth open. When he finally looked ready to speak, three clicks came from the door behind him, letting them know that Blake was coming back in. As the door swung open, Fang and the wolf ducked out, leaving Blake to shut the door after sneering at the two captives left in the cell.

"Here," said Hayden, sliding the second bowl of porridge closer to Riley. She stretched to grab it and sat back up against the wall, gazing at Hayden – the boy who had the ability to heal.

"How did you do that?" she asked weakly.

"I don't know," he said truthfully. "I just can."

"Are you some sort of monster or something?" she asked hesitantly.

Hayden's breathing shuddered again. He looked away for a moment while Riley kept her eyes on him. Feeling that she had crossed a line, she quickly jumped to the next question that came to her. "Have you ever gotten out?"

"No," he said, bowing his head. He turned his sad eyes to her.

For someone who could cure his own wounds, he looked to be in so much pain. "Why do they make you do that?" she asked, nodding her head at his wrist.

"Because they can't kill me," he said simply.

Riley wiped the sleep from her eyes and looked out the barred window at the glow of a rising sun. She nodded and brushed her bangs behind her ear.

"Well they can," he added quickly. "They're just scared that if I die, I'll..." he paused as he pinched the bridge of his nose. "They just think that I'll be free if I leave this body."

"So they think you'll live forever?" she asked, outraged at Zahid's stupidity.

Hayden took another wavering breath and looked away. Riley could see that his eyes were forced shut, most likely fighting back tears that were determined to escape. She hugged her knees tightly as she hunched forward. She too felt the immense pressure build in her throat.

The thing she hated most about being locked up was the silence. She had never heard such quiet and hated the way it allowed her to think. She was able to concentrate on everything that came to her thoughts, and her mind spun with questions. *Peck, what happened to him? Parker, did she notice? Would anyone have noticed that I've disappeared? Would anyone know that my time to join Craig, Amanda, the poor man in the newspaper, the cab driver, and the two people I watched die in last night's dream is probably closer than anyone could have expected?*

She rested her head on her knees while Hayden watched her from his dark corner. For what seemed like hours, they sat in complete silence. Her ears began to ring when, finally, Hayden spoke.

"What's it like, you know, out there?" he asked as he shuffled around in his corner.

"Well," she said, thinking about the world she had been taken from. "It's big." Her voice shook. "There are a lot of people. Some of them are nice, I guess, and others are complete assholes." She was now secretly referring to the only people she knew. "Um, it's sometimes scary," she sighed and sat up to look into his dark brown eyes. "It can be beautiful too."

Hayden listened as though she was telling a story. He laid his head on his knees, which he hugged tightly, imagining a world he had never seen. "Could you tell me about rain?" he asked with excitement, seeming to have found hidden strength.

"Well it's..." she stopped herself and stared at Hayden. He was actually smiling. "You don't know what rain is?" she asked. The boy shook his head. "You've never seen it through the widow?" She pointed up at the sky, and again Hayden's head shook.

"This part of the valley doesn't get it," he explained. "I've heard the villagers don't like it."

"Hayden," she said smirking, "you must have seen it, like it's impossible that you haven't. Rain is just the water that falls from the sky in a bunch of little droplets." He stared at her blankly, waiting for her to continue. "Really, Hayden?"

"I've only heard about it," he explained, his eyes looking sad again.

"You heard?" her eyes widened. "They don't like you, at all, do they?" she asked. Hayden shook his head and buried his face in his knees. "Well does anyone here treat you decently? Someone has to teach you. I mean, you speak kind of like they do. You had to learn that somewhere."

Hayden looked back at her. "I was taught to speak like you do so that you'd understand."

Riley pushed her bangs behind her ear once again and stared at him, bewildered. "What? Who taught you to do that?"

"The man in my head," he said quietly. He shuffled in his corner uncomfortably on the concrete floor.

Riley, now sunken into the corner, was at a loss for words. *The voice in our heads must be linked in some way.* She sat in her thoughts and pondered about the interesting yet frightening being that spoke to both of them. The voice had taught Hayden to speak and had somewhat loosely instructed her on where to go and what to do.

The door clicked three times, and Fang entered the concrete room. He was alone this time and carried a large, freshly-picked lettuce head and a couple of red tomatoes on a plate. He slammed the door shut. Keeping an eye on Hayden, he slowly placed the food onto the floor and backed away to where Riley sat in her corner.

"Has he hurt you?" Fang asked in a whisper, crouching low to face her.

"No," she hissed, looking disgusted. "Honestly, Fang," she snapped, "do you believe us or that monkey ass, Zahid?" she asked, nodding to the door.

"I couldn't talk with you while my brother was around," he tried to explain, but Riley quickly jumped up to her feet and began to examine the tools on the wall.

"You know, Fang, I didn't see your brother at all today. And I didn't see anyone when you had your couple minutes alone with us." She spun around to find him standing behind her. He was still a full inch shorter than Riley in height.

"Brothers, Riley," he said. "I've got brothers: Ambro and Blake."

Riley lifted a hand between them, making Fang recoil as she shoved a knife into his palm. "Why don't you try it!" she hissed and shoved him aside.

She stood at the opposite wall and watched Fang, who seemed to be frozen on spot. Before she knew it, Fang turned around and sliced his hand with the knife. Her jaw dropped, but she quickly regained control and glared at him.

"And that's as much as I'll do. I don't have any healing powers," he said. He looked at the scrawny body in dirty brown clothes that sat in the corner.

Hayden shifted uncomfortably once again, and his breath shuddered.

"What do you want, Fang?" she snapped.

"I just want to say..." he drew a breath and looked her straight in the eyes. "Well, I want to believe you."

"Yeah?" she stared at him as he hung the knife back onto a hook in the wall. "Well it's the truth. He's no devil. He's just a child." Riley pointed at Hayden and marched up to Fang. She straightened up tall to tower over him, her nostrils flaring. "And I'm no follower. I'm just a person you've abducted." Fang's bottom lip twitched, and he looked away from her and toward Hayden. The small boy sat in the dark, watching them closely. "Fang, if you did believe me, then you'd help us get out."

Chapter 14

◇ ◇ ◇

"No," Fang said, looking disgusted at the thought. "I am not doing that, Riley."

Riley's eyes sharpened. Fang stared back at her, nostrils flaring, and his eyes darted from Riley to Hayden. He shook his head. "Not doing it. Do you know what they'd do to me?"

"Take away your special clothing privileges?" she jeered.

"Riley," he said, exasperated. He took a step closer and raised his hands at her before dropping them again as he became conscious of his actions. "They will find out that I helped you and then kill me."

She leaned back against the scratched-up wall. Her nostrils were still flaring angrily as she looked away from Fang, who held a key in his fist. She did not want to spend the rest of her life trapped in a room. She wanted out. She slid down into a sitting position against the wall and fell silent as Fang stared down at her. His fists trembled, and his eyes darted nervously around the room. He took one last deep breath, shoved the key into the keyhole, and twisted it to make the familiar three clicking noises. He pulled it open and slammed it closed on his way out.

Riley hoped Fang had given in and would "forget" to lock the door, but her heart sank when she heard three more clicks, letting her know that he was not going to help. She sat the base of the door in hopes that she was wrong, but no key slid underneath.

She planted her face into her hands and tugged tightly on her bangs that were hooked between her fingers. She straightened back up when she thought she heard Hayden scratching at the wall, but he was not moving. Hayden sat quietly, his bloodshot eyes watching her with a blank expression. She followed the noise until her ears led her to the wall opposite from her. It was the wall she had attacked the night before. Every mark she had made on it was falling off. The scratches were turning into a grey powder and dropping to the cement floor, leaving a flat surface behind.

"I don't understand," said Hayden, shutting his eyes tightly while Riley brushed her hair back and stared at the now unmarked wall with wide eyes.

"Me neither," she mumbled and looked at him. A ball formed in her throat as she stared into the boy's sad eyes.

"No," he said quietly. "I don't understand why you can't get us out."

"Hayden, do you not see what I'm trying to do?" she questioned, trying to keep calm. Her hands were raised and her fingers clawed at the wall.

"But he said it would be easy for you." His bottom lip quivered.

"The man in your head," she said simply while nodding. She fought back the force of her tears, which were more powerful than ever. She thought she was going crazy; perhaps she already was.

"Yes," he whispered.

"Ok. Now why don't you ask him how in hell I am supposed to easily get out of here with you?"

He shook his head weakly. "He just told me to wait and not hurt myself," he said. "I've been waiting for you for a very long time, White Witch. Please, I just want it to stop," he sniffed.

"Why do you call me that?" she shot.

"It's what he calls you," he explained in his weak tone.

"My name is Riley Orel. If I'm anything other than myself, I'm probably the Nightwatcher – whatever the hell that is!"she said.

They fell silent while they ate what they could of the vegetables Fang had brought for them and piled their dirty dishes in a corner once they had finished. The rest of the long day was spent in utter silence while Riley stared at the grey powder that had piled up on the floor by the now smooth wall.

Once night had fallen through the window and into the cell, three clicks were heard from the metallic door. Fang entered alone and shut the door behind him, dropping more vegetables onto the ground. Without a word, he picked up the stack of dirty dishes and left the room after glancing over at Riley and giving a small crooked smile.

Riley did not move. She glared at him as he gently shut the door. Hayden, who had already begun eating a baby carrot, shoved a plate her way. She took a breath and ate what she could before stacking the plates in the corner.

Seek them out, and protect him. She shut her eyes as the man's voice resonated in her head. The image of the metallic door that locked them in their cement room was clear in her imagination and was all she could picture. In her mind, she opened the door and turned left into the cozy room behind the glass doors. She opened her eyes and looked at Hayden, who was gazing at the metallic door as if waiting for something.

His eyes caught hers, and they sprang to their feet. "The clicks!" they both shot together.

"I didn't hear them," she said, a rush of adrenaline coming over her.

"He's letting us?" he asked as quietly as he could with the same anxious tone.

Riley looked to the door. *Would Fang let us escape? Would he put everything on the line to save us? Is this some sort of trap?* All she had to do was pull on the handle to find their answer.

She gently placed her hand on the cold silver handle and grasped it tightly. Her breathing quivered as Hayden approached her and nodded. With all her force, she swung the metallic door open, revealing a dark and empty cement hallway lined with crates along the walls.

They exited the cell and shut the door behind them. Before taking any more steps into the hall, she turned left and opened the glass door. Hayden followed after her, shutting the door quietly behind them and looked at Riley, who walked around the carpeted room. He was clearly confused but kept quiet, thinking that she knew what she was doing.

On top of the desk, opposite from the door, lay very familiar clothes which Riley had not seen since the day Fang and Rocky took her from her home. Her yellow shirt with the red diagonal stripe was sprawled out on top of papers and calendars. Her jeans were folded neatly and placed on the edge of the desk by pencils and other writing tools. She picked up her clothes, and before she could turn to Hayden to ask him for privacy, something caught her eye. Across the room was a sitting area, complete with two reddish-brown leather loveseats which faced one another. Beside the fireplace, the wall behind the seats was lined in bookshelves completely filled with books. On a three foot high pillar, surrounded by the chairs and shelves, sat a glass container which enclosed a large dark brown leather book.

She made her way to the glass container and pulled off the lid to get a closer look at what it held. She placed the lid on the carpeted ground and pulled out the old book. The cover read *Book of the Witches*. The title was written in someone's handwriting, and nothing more marked the outer cover of the book. Underneath the writing, there was a clear gemstone pressed into the cover. A golden chain wrapped around the rock umpteen times. Riley tapped the gem a couple times – it seemed real. She let the clothes tucked beneath her arm drop to the floor and opened the book to flip through the blank pages it held.

A sudden desire for the useless book rushed over her as inaudible words echoed lightly in her ears. Her fingers buzzed with excitement, and her heart leapt with joy as she held the object of her desires in her hands. She picked the clothes up off the floor and turned to Hayden. Without speaking, he seemed to understand what she meant. He turned away while she quickly changed out of the tattered nightgown and into her own clothes.

Nothing but the book occupied her mind as a light smile formed upon her face. She carried the book carefully over to the desk as though it were a delicate baby. Finding a single strapped bag, she emptied all of its contents onto the desk, making Hayden gasp with disagreement. Riley ignored him and tucked the book into the bag. Edging out of the room through the glass door, she looked for signs of movement in the hallway, but nothing was around. With the strange book by her side, Riley felt her luck changing. She felt like she was about to escape.

Hayden and Riley made their way to the front door of the metallic building without a hitch. They each pressed an ear against the door but could not hear any sound coming from outside. They pushed the door ajar, leaving but enough room for both of them to see into the quiet and lifeless grounds. They walked out into the quiet yard, tiptoeing their way to the edge of the forest on their left.

The village, from what they could see, was calm and quiet. The full moon hung directly above them, and the stars sparkled across the black sky. If she was not determined to escape a world that held her kidnapped, she would have thought of her surroundings as the most incredible piece of work she could ever catch on camera.

After giving the Valley of Hay one last look and giving a nod of unrecognized thanks for Fang's help, Riley and Hayden jumped into the forest. They walked a dozen feet into the forest and turned to circle the village, looking for a trail. Although Riley was collected with the book at her side, she could see the forest beast reappearing in her imagination. With her guard up, they continued on, dedicated to changing their futures.

"Thank you," panted Hayden while they walked the perimeter of the village beyond the group of trees that kept them hidden. "I've been waiting forever for this day, you know."

"Yeah, it's fine," she said to him as she stepped over a dead tree on the ground. For a while, they walked in silence with nothing but the crunching of twigs and leaves on the ground making noise with each step.

After a while, they stopped to take a break. "You think we've made it around the village yet?" asked Hayden hopefully.

"Maybe half," she estimated Hayden's expression went blank as he sat on the dark log closest to him. Riley leaned up against a tree as she looked through the forest toward the silent village.

"Um, Riley?" came Hayden's voice from within the darkness surrounding them.

"Yes?" she said blankly as she stared at what looked like a torch lit far in the distance.

"I'm scared," he said, looking away as she turned to face him.

She slid down the tree and sat up against it on the ground. She glanced at him curiously. "Well, when I was little, my dad, he used to tell me to hum or whistle when I'd get scared. Why not try that?" She was shocked at Hayden's reaction. His eyes widened, and his head and voice shook, terrified.

"You never whistle while alone in a forest," he said seriously. "Under no circumstances."

Riley stared back at him. "Well, you're not alone, but you're right. We should get further away."

"They'll hear," he said quietly. He stood up onto his feet. "Why don't we go now? Why are we circling the Valley of Hay?"

"I'm looking for a road," she explained. "And just so you know, I really doubt that they'll hear us once we've got a couple kilometers between us and them." She nodded her head to the village over the trees.

"There's no road," he said in a risen temper. "And they can hear and do weird things," he added through clenched teeth. "Why can't we just leave now?" he begged.

"Not tonight. When it's dark, we can't travel through the forest," she said, picturing the beast running with the wolves.

Before Hayden had a chance to retort, a twig snapped a couple dozen feet into the forest. Riley anxiously grabbed to pull Hayden back, and heard another snap followed by a muffled thud. They could hear deep breaths that quivered in the dark forest. Riley ushered Hayden away along the edge of the trees.

"What was that? Hayden whispered anxiously when they had gotten far enough from the sounds.

"I don't know," she lied and continued to walk as more lights hovered around the village.

"Do you think they know?" he asked after following her gaze toward the village lights. They gained speed as they peered through the trees at the many torch lights. Before she had time to answer, a deep yell resonated from the opposite end of the village. People began to shout and howls erupted. Riley's eyes widened as she grabbed hold of Hayden's shoulder. She pulled him deeper into the trees while keeping a sharp eye on everything around them.

"Crap! Crap! Crap!" she repeated as she was forced to hurry deeper into the forest. Her eyes darted in every direction while Hayden focused on running forward on his weak legs. The screaming and howling got louder and sounded as though it was following them.

She ran after Hayden with the bag tucked under her arm, the strap over her shoulders, and the thought of the beast continuously running through her mind. She ran faster and faster. Just like in her dream, she was getting tired and began to pant, but no wolves followed her from behind. She looked over her shoulder and suddenly ran into Hayden, who had come to an abrupt stop. They fell to the ground with muffled thuds and the sound of snapping twigs under their bodies.

Riley lifted her head, and to her horror, a wheezing shadow creature stood in front of her against a dead oak tree. Its pale green fingers pierced the tree's bark while its birdlike feet gripped the broken branches and the rocks which it stood on. Its hooded head lifted to look at Riley and Hayden, who lay petrified on the ground. The shadow creature took a deep breath, looked up to the starry sky through the cluster of trees branches, and let out a piercing screech which made both Riley and Hayden cover their ears and roll uncontrollably in the dirt.

When the screeching stopped, the shadow creature pulled its hand from the tree and made its way to Riley. It hunched down to look at her before it suddenly straightened up and began to look nervously throughout the woods. After swinging its head around to check every direction, the creature retreated into the dark.

As the buzzing in her ears died down, the barking of wolves in the distance became clear to Riley, and she jumped to her feet without hesitation, pulling Hayden up with her. They ran at full speed until she tripped on a root and slammed onto the ground. She looked over her shoulder once again and could see figures running toward them in the distant moonlight. She pulled herself up and began to run as fast as she could. Seconds into her sprint, she realised that something was not right; Hayden was missing. She could not stop running, but looked around frantically for him. Dodging trees, she looked back over her shoulder and saw what she had feared the most: the beast.

Dark eyes gleamed in the shadows among a pack of grey wolves. She forced herself to run faster, her hair flying in and out of her eyes and her arms working at full speed. The ground began to tremble as the beast got closer. It was over; she knew what happened next. She began to slow down as the beast caught up to her. Just as in her dream, the black, hairy arm swung around her and dragged her deeper into the forest. She was too terrified to look it in the eye. Her struggle for escape was futile; it was too strong. "Let me go!" she screamed. Then it occurred to her that Hayden, the boy she had sworn to protect, was now alone in the forest, left for certain punishment by the villagers and wolves. "No!" she screamed. She ached to break free and save the boy that had been waiting for her for twelve years.

The beast's grip tightened as it ran faster and suddenly jumped into a bush to wait for the pack of wolves to pass them by. The beast covered Riley's mouth to prevent her from making any noise. She breathed unsteadily through her nose as the beast stood up against a tree. It seemed to be listening for their followers. Riley fought to look up at the beast and, finally, after loosening her grip on its arms, the beast mimicked her by loosening its grip, allowing her to look at its long-snouted face. Its lengthy black whiskers stuck out from the sides of its long nose, and sharp, sparkling white teeth protruded from its mouth. Black pointed ears fixed themselves on what sounded like footsteps coming up from behind them.

Riley struggled to see what the source of the noise was, but the beast's grip tightened, and she was forced to do nothing but listen quietly.

"Have you found the boy?" spoke Zahid's deep voice. Riley's eyes widened.

"No," said a woman who sounded to be coming from the opposite direction.

"And the girl?" growled Zahid.

"She isn't anywhere either, sir."

Riley could hear Zahid stomping around angrily and muttering to himself. "Can no one else pick up their sent?"

"The boy has none," whispered Blake's voice. At this, the beast's grip tightened once more, and Riley was lifted from the ground.

"He could be hiding right here beneath our noses and we still wouldn't be able to find him," added the woman.

"I know, but what I mean is, I don't understand why I can't find the girl" Zahid said angrily.

"We had her," said the woman. "Fang caught up and must have masked her sent. We have no idea where he went with her."

Riley's eyes fell onto the beast's black, hairy hands that covered her mouth.

"Don't you dare say that!" yelled Blake. "My brother understands the importance of their capture! He would never turn his back on us!"

"But what frustrates me, Blake," said Zahid, "is how they managed to escape even with all of the enchantments placed upon the chamber."

"I have no idea, sir," said Blake.

"Well, was it not you who had to bring the nightfall meal to the prisoners?"

"Well, yes but—"

"But what?" interrupted Zahid.

"I had forgotten to feed them," he said shamefully.

"Now," said Zahid, with a slightly calmer disposition, "the skeleton key is the only tool that will allow anyone access to the Devil's resting room. Am I not correct?"

"Of course but—"

"Then tell me how in hell they managed to escape if you were the only person with the key in their possession!" shouted Zahid.

"The girl," said the woman's voice. "The girl has powers none of us could imagine, sir. She probably broke the spells placed on the chamber."

"Speaking of powers," said Blake, "I have seen deeper into the forest than this. Sir, it's dying. The creatures are making their way through," he said in an anxious tone.

The beast's grip on her mouth tightened even more. She wanted to whimper as the pain was excruciating. She was held up against the beast, trembling, her arms wrapped together beneath the beast's second arm. "I am well aware of that," she heard Zahid say. "Continue your search, and Father Monsignor of Fallsdale has another witch we can use for the forest. She will come in with the next shipment of tools and fabrics." Riley could hear their footsteps shuffling away and suddenly stop. "And if you find Fang, I wish to have a word with him," Zahid added and then took off.

Riley was held in spot for a couple of minutes after the three villagers had left. The beast sniffed loudly, pointing its long, black-haired nose in every direction. Its grip loosened, freeing Riley, and she took a few quick steps forward before turning around and tripping over another root in the ground.

She panted while staring at the beast in front of her – the beast which had hid her from Zahid and the others. It bowed its head. She knew running would be futile, so she pulled herself up against a tree and looked curiously at the monster that was sadly gazing into her eyes. The wolf-like creature whimpered and turned away. She had not noticed before, but it wore dark blue jeans that tore at the seams, and its enormous feet ripped through the ends of a pair of shoes.

The beast was tall, slim, and toned but still looked weak as it held at tree branches for support with its gigantic clawed hands. Riley gaped at the beast with an open mouth. She did not understand why it had not yet killed her.

She approached it cautiously. It breathed heavily and stared up at the moon through the tree branches overhead. Her breath shuddered as she stood only three feet away. The beast snorted and turned to look at her with its big, brown, gleaming eyes. It sat down against the tree and extended two hands to grasp one of hers. It held her hand gently and let go as she dropped to her knees.

"Fang?" she said through trembling lips. "Is that you?" she whispered, trying to hold back her shaky voice.

The beast looked away for a moment. Its eyes were pressed shut, and she saw its head nod once before looking back at her. Her breath quivered, and she wiped her sleepy eyes.

"What happened?" she asked in a shaky voice. "What did they do to you?"

The beast looked up to the stars and pointed upwards with a large, clawed index finger.

She breathed deeply as she looked up to the moon behind him. "Oh my god," she sniffed. "A werewolf? They're real too?" she added as she pinched the bridge of her nose.

The beast stared back at her and nodded softly, looking ashamed. Its sharp black ears lowered as it bowed its head. They sat in their own thoughts. Fang's panting was all that made noise while Riley tried to process the events of the night. *What happened to Hayden? What would they do to him? Would I ever see the boy who placed all his hopes in me again?* Her questions were still as numerous as the stars.

Chapter 15

◊ ◊ ◊

Riley watched Fang in his beast form as he sat in silence. His ears focused as he looked around and occasionally sniffed the cool air. She brushed back her hair and sat up against the tree opposite from Fang.

"So," she said, breaking the silence. "Are you like this forever?" she asked hesitantly and watched him closely, noticing how even in the form of a giant wolf, his features still held some human resemblance.

His head shook vigorously as he reached an index up toward the moon.

"You'll be normal in the morning? Like in the movies?"

Tilting a hairy hand to one side and back to the other, he gestured *kind of*. He sighed through his long black nose and looked over his shoulder, abruptly jumping onto all fours and growling in the direction from where Zahid and the two others had left. He stood up onto his hind legs and sniffed the air. He looked back at Riley with uncertainty painted across his monstrous face and continued to search.

Riley mimicked him and walked by his side. "What is it?" she asked, staring into the distance. Suddenly, she heard twigs snapping on the ground. She took a step back while Fang went forward.

Riley watched a figure coming into focus from the shadows of the trees, and before she recognized who it was, Fang stepped backward and sat against his tree. Hayden came barrelling toward Riley. He was panting heavily and had cuts across his face that healed once he took a seat on the ground by Riley's feet. She immediately sunk down to grasp him, happy to see he was safe.

"Where were you? What happened?" she asked, worry coating her words.

Hayden opened his mouth, but before he could speak, he noticed Fang sitting in the dark and jumped to his feet in fright. He pointed, lost for words, and began to back up while reaching to pull Riley to safety.

She grabbed his hand and pulled him back down to the ground. "It's alright," she assured him. "It's Fang," she added. The beast shuffled around in the dark at her words. "Where were you?" she repeated and grabbed Hayden by his head to force his focus on her instead of the beast.

"I turned around to help you when you fell," he panted quickly. "I didn't notice that you were gone, but when I turned around to come back for you, you ran passed me," he explained. "You were looking straight at me and then took off without saying anything. That's when I saw…" he trailed off and turned again to look at the beast behind Riley. "I saw him and the wolves, and they never even noticed me. I tried following them to find you, but I was too slow. I saw the man that always came into my cell and a woman. I thought they spotted me and I panicked, but they just walked right by. Then I kept running until I got here."

"I didn't see you," she said confusedly. "Hayden…"

At that moment, Fang sprang to his clawed feet. He ran up to them and began to circle them angrily. Riley and Hayden both stood up slowly while watching him hiss at something they could not see. Before Riley had time to speak, she noticed what had caused Fang to act this way. Half a dozen shadow creatures had been making their way closer to them from every direction. Two of the creatures hovered above the ground, and the rest crept over on their birdlike feet.

Riley, Fang, and Hayden found themselves back to back in the circle of shadow creatures that approached at a slow pace. Fang growled as Riley reached back to make sure Hayden was still by her side. Fang swiftly pounced at one of the hovering shadow creatures. To Riley's surprise, he did not fall through the creature but was able to claw and bite at every part of it.

Riley turned around to find a shadow creature limping her way, raising its pale green hand to strike. She quickly grabbed hold of its raised wrist and attempted to pull it down. She grabbed the second rising hand, and with all her force, she pulled the arms down and pushed the creature to the ground. Riley turned on spot to find Hayden being lifted by his arms by a hovering shadow creature. She threw herself at the creature but fell through it. "No!" she shouted as she tried to stop the hovering creature from harming Hayden, but she could not touch it.

Another limping shadow creature grabbed her by the arms. She pulled forward and broke free from it. Falling toward the ground, she closed her grip around Hayden's dangling legs. She pulled hard, forcing herself back onto the ground, but nothing she did would stop the hovering shadow creature. Out of nowhere, Fang suddenly leapt at the creature that held Hayden and bit its throat, causing it to screech and drop Hayden, who fell onto Riley.

Riley and Hayden covered their ears to block out the piercing screech. Riley rolled onto her back as the sound caused her so much pain. The screeching stopped as Fang let go of the creature and dropped it to the ground. It was left motionless as Fang continued to fight off the creatures that crept closer. Riley staggered to her feet and swung a fist at a footed creature. With a loud smack, it stammered backward.

Hayden also got to his feet and held back a grounded creature while Fang clawed at it. Three shadow creatures now lay motionless on the ground, and the others became hesitant and slowly backed away. Riley, panting, made her way to Hayden, whose scrapes across his face were not yet healed.

Fang growled and hissed as he began to circle around, scaring off the remaining shadow creatures. Before anything else could be taken in, howls erupted from the village. Even in his beast form, Fang's features showed a worried expression that told Riley that it was time to move.

With the shadow creatures long gone, they were able to run safely through the dark forest, but they could not get far enough from the sounds of the howling wolves trailing them from behind. Riley ran with all of her force, followed closely behind by Hayden. The cuts across his face still bled, and crimson droplets ran down his cheeks as he continued forward. Fang ran slowly on all fours so that he was close enough to both Riley and Hayden.

The trees were getting thinner and more spread out, and all color was lost in this part of the forest. Trees had fallen over, and everything looked lifeless. Riley jumped over a rotten log and continued to sprint with Hayden at her side, hopeful that they were going to make it out.

The howling from further back eventually ceased, and the sky lightened. Riley watched Fang closely, waiting for him to transform as the daylight approached, but he still seemed active as a beast. Fang seemed eager to escape this form as well. His big, brown eyes met hers as they began to slow their pace.

Hayden panted while looking from Riley to Fang. They stood quietly for a moment to catch their breath when Fang, suddenly, wandered away on all fours. He had been gone for no more than a couple of seconds when he reappeared from behind a bush in his normal human form. He stood, once again, an inch shorter than Riley and yet slightly taller than Hayden.

"You helped us," Hayden panted. "Thank you." He stared at Fang, who watched him cautiously and nodded after a short moment's ponder. Riley looked into Fang's brown eyes, feeling overwhelmed with gratitude toward him. She smiled lightly, and he acknowledged it with a smirk before turning around quickly to ensure their safety.

"Ok," said Fang, his voice as steady and powerful as always. "We have to get out of here."

He buttoned his ripped jeans and walked past Riley, who was bent over, still panting. Hayden straightened up and watched Fang lead the way. "Why did he help us?" he whispered to Riley.

Riley turned toward Fang, who walked shirtless through the thin group of dead trees. *Why had he helped us? Why would he help something that his people believed to be the most dangerous thing in the world?* Riley shrugged her shoulders and followed.

"So," she said after a moment of silence, "you change when the moon is out?"

"Kind of," he said simply, sounding ashamed.

Riley looked up to the slightly lighter sky. The moon and stars were hidden away by thick clouds, and further on was a dim light, telling her that day was approaching. The air got cooler as they made their way farther from the Valley of Hay. Hayden's heavy breath was visible in the air, and the cuts were not yet completely dried on his face.

Riley brushed her bangs out of her face and made a mental note to chop them off at the next chance she got. She stepped cautiously overtop of broken twigs and sharp rocks with her bare feet and wondered how long it would be until she would reach a place that she recognized.

"Here," came Fang's voice. He held up a pair of destroyed sneakers. She smiled at him.

"Thank you," she said.

They seemed to walk for hours in silence. The only thing that made sound was the cracking of branches and leaves on the ground and their lungs harshly exhaling the cool air. The sun's light had now reached its way farther across the sky and peered through the clouds overhead. Not one soul seemed to live in these woods. No birds chirped overhead; no squirrels ran around. There was not even a single mosquito in the air. The intense grey light from the clouds blocking the sun made everything frightening, and it seemed like a possible situation for another attack by shadow creatures.

Riley wondered if Fang knew what he was doing but could not summon up the courage to ask. She followed quietly, when finally, Fang stopped and turned to face them. He made nervous eye contact before speaking. "This is where we forget where we are," he explained to them.

Riley looked to Hayden, who donned the same confused expression as herself, and turned back to Fang as he continued. "There is a reason why the Valley of Hay is the safest place in the world," he said calmly and pointed around the decaying forest. "There are enchantments all around us. Anyone who leaves the boundaries of the forest's protected area will forget the way from which they came, and anyone who tries getting back into the village will walk directly around it."

Riley and Hayden nodded slowly, and Fang took another glance around the dead forest. Fang took a deep breath and then looked back at them. "There are going to be more of those shadow creatures once we leave this place," he said. He looked at Hayden, who seemed to be debating whether or not to speak.

"Does it really matter?" Hayden asked quickly, looking away from Fang's glare. "I mean, they can get into the valley. They won't be stuck out here, so why should we be worrying about them out here?"

"The creatures in the forest that were by the entrance to the

Valley of Hay got lucky and broke through the enchantments," he said simply. "There are many more of them, and next time, most of them could be at their strongest. This means that you'll be in bigger danger."

"At their strongest?" asked Riley.

"When they fly, human flesh can't touch them," he explained.

"So they have a weakness!" Riley exclaimed. Fang turned to her with a worried expression.

"Yes," he said slowly, "but that's what's confusing."

"You don't know what's causing them to walk?" she asked in a whisper, feeling anxious.

"No, I do," he assured her. She gave a breath of relief. "I just don't understand how they let themselves become weakened like that. They gain their strength by feeding off of life, and the mortal world has got lots of that."

Fang continued to nervously look over his shoulders as he spoke. His frightened eyes made Riley's stomach turn. Her breath shuddered. "I don't know anything about these things except that they don't like me," she said as she tried finding Fang's eyes with her own.

"They don't like anyone," he said, shaking his head. "These creatures only care for themselves." His temper built as he expressed his disgust for the creatures.

Hayden slowly turned to face them, his bare toes now gripping the cold dirt. "But where are they coming from?" Riley asked as her eyes followed Hayden's movements.

"They come from a really dark place," said Fang. Hayden took a couple of steps forward. "Some call it Hell, but my people call it by its real name." Riley's attention was now focused on nothing but Fang. "The Shadow World."

Riley's mouth widened, and her excitement grew at the possibility of having Fang answer some of her many questions. Before she could ask anything, Hayden interrupted them. "Guys," he said. His voice brought Riley back to her senses. "Can you feel that?"

Fang instinctively turned on spot and, his eyes began to scan every direction. Riley could see the fear on his face as his eyes darted from left to right. "You can only transform at night, right?" she asked as something scurried by in her peripheral vision.

"That's a lie," he said, and he beckoned them closer to him with his hand. He had Riley and Hayden follow close behind while they traveled further away from the village. The fine hairs on the back of Riley's neck stood up, and she became completely disoriented. She forgot where the Valley of Hay had been. Although she was pretty certain they had travelled straight the entire time, she was unsure about the point which they had been running from.

Alongside Hayden and Fang, she began to notice dark figures moving through her peripherals, but she could not catch them dead on when she turned to get a better look. For the most part, the creatures were fast and stayed out of sight. All of a sudden, one large shadow creature came charging at them from the opposite direction. It flew a foot from the ground and stopped in front of them to growl at the heavens. Black, tangible-looking smoke lifted off of its cloak. Fang lunged toward the creature's chest, turned into his beast form in mid air, and knocked the creature to the ground. He growled and bit at his enemy, and the creature beneath him hissed and clawed back. Riley spun around to find dozens of shadow creatures hovering their way toward them. "We can't touch them," she said anxiously as one charged her way.

Riley dropped to the ground, missed the shadow creature's attack by inches, and rolled over as another pale green hand slashed down toward her head. Again she rolled, and Fang continued to intervene, knocking the shadow creatures to the ground where he beat on them with his large claws. Breathless, Riley jumped to her feet and ran to Hayden.

The shadow creatures advanced on them from every direction. While Fang attacked two at once, Riley and Hayden stood back to back, both shaking and hoping for a way out. Hayden shivered and sank to his knees. A shadow creature pressed him to the ground by his shoulders. Riley swung for its head, but nothing except cool air made contact with her fist. The creature lifted its head and hissed at her. It wrapped two long, pale grey hands around her shoulders and threw her back. She skidded across the ground until her back hit a thin, dead tree. She lifted herself back up onto her numb legs and walked with a limp over to the creatures that now hovered in front of Hayden.

Fang snapped the neck of another shadow creature, making it screech painfully. Riley immediately fell to the ground to cover her ears. She could see the largest of the shadow creatures hovering in front of Hayden. It was breathing heavily, its chest beneath the cloak growing then shrinking at a quick pace. Its hands tightened their grip on Hayden's shoulders, and he let out a cry. The surrounding shadow creatures lifted their sharp, pale green claws and readied themselves to strike. A sudden and unexpected screech filled the forest, and the shadow creature that had been gripping onto Hayden's shoulders let go of him and flew away. The creature disappeared into the dead forest, and the remaining creatures only stared curiously at the weeping boy. One by one, they glided away until the only creatures left were the charcoal black remains of Fang's victims.

Chapter 16

"They've left," said Fang, shrinking back to his human form and buckling his unbuttoned jeans. "Why would they leave?" He stared off into the direction the creatures had run to. Confusion was splashed across his face. "What did you do to it?" he asked Hayden anxiously with wide gleaming eyes.

"I—I don't know," Hayden replied nervously.

Fang turned away, looking sulky. "I have never heard of anything frightening enough to make a group like that run away – especially when they were just about to win the fight," said Fang. "They were winning," he repeated.

Hayden lifted himself onto his feet and looked at Fang, who still hoped for an answer. Riley could see the cuts beneath the dry blood smeared across Hayden's face. She wondered why they had not yet healed but was distracted by the sound of tweeting birds flying overhead. In that moment, she realized that the woods did not seem quite as dead anymore. She could see green plants growing happily a couple yards ahead. Excitement erupted in the pit of her stomach, and she began to walk toward the green patch without caution. Fang and Hayden, who thought she had seen something important, watchfully followed after her.

"What is it?" whispered Fang.

"It's nothing," she said as she looked at the bushes ahead. "It's just that... it's cold." She felt the earth with her bare toes that poked through the holes in Fang's mangled shoes.

"Of course it is," replied Fang, looking puzzled at her confusion. "We have left the valley."

She exhaled, her white breath slowly dispersing into the chilly air. Hayden stood straight up on the frozen soil in his raggedy clothes. His soft gaze rested on Riley's face. "What now?" he asked innocently.

"I'll take you two through the forest," said Fang, his furrowed eyebrows giving away the feelings of anxiousness that he was obviously trying to hide. "After that," he paused, "well, I don't know. We'll have another few hours of walking, I believe." Riley drew a breath of relief. "The priests didn't want to have too much trouble finding the Valley of Hay on every visit," he continued. They walked closer to the lively part of the woods which the shadow creatures had not touched.

"You were put there?" Riley asked. They walked into the green-filled section of the forest and stood beneath a large patch of dark green spruce trees that seemed to go on for miles ahead.

"Hundreds of years ago, yes," he replied and pushed a branch out of his face. They walked on over the cold dirt as more birds flew above them.

"Because you could change?" she asked.

"No." Fang looked at Hayden and stopped. "Him," He turned his focus to the ground and continued to walk, looking upset.

Riley stopped to let Fang and Hayden take a couple steps ahead. The air began to chill. "He's only fourteen," she muttered, not daring to look Fang in the eyes.

"More like a couple hundred," added Fang calmly.

"Several," whispered Hayden's voice, and Riley looked up to his shameful eyes.

"Oh my god," she said quietly and shook her head twice. Her eyes weakened as she looked from Fang to Hayden for confirmation. She did not want to believe that the boy could be so old. She did not want to believe she had been misguided. If there were invisible circles in the world, enchantments, shadow creatures, and wolf men, she felt it would be stupid not to believe in this possibility as well. "Are you really?" Her voice and body trembled. Hayden nodded.

"We should keep going," suggested Fang. Riley nodded.

Their walk along the frozen ground continued. They passed beneath the dark green trees until large mountains with frosty white peaks came into view. They rested while Fang wandered around and looked into the distance at a valley full of life and water about fifty feet downhill.

Riley sat on top of a large rock. She hoped for a voice to echo in her mind and give her some direction, but nothing came.

"There's something I've been meaning to ask you," said Fang as he appeared from behind a branch. He walked up to Hayden's side and sat on the ground against a tree. Looking at Riley, he exhaled loudly. "The night on which you confided to Fallsdale's priest about the shadow creatures following you, was the night I was sent to watch over you. I was supposed to ensure that we wouldn't be protecting someone who was not in need." Riley nodded as she had already known about this. "We, Rocky and I, kept our distance. We probably shouldn't have."

"I tracked you down into the forest in Georgia, I believe." His eyes sharpened as he tried to remember everything from that night. "When we finally found you, men and women in uniform were picking you and two others up off the ground." He stared deep into her eyes, not allowing a break in contact. "How did you escape the shadow creature that night?" he asked, shaking his head in confusion. "I mean, something happened. When Rocky and I found it, it was writhing in pain and eventually died."

Riley drew a breath and looked into Fang's big brown eyes. "The hat-man saved me," she answered. Fang's head tilted slightly.

"Who is the hat-man?" he asked. Hayden straightened up and listened intently as though he was being told a bedtime story.

"He's something," she said after a moment's thought. "He's a creature. I don't know exactly what he is."

"What does he look like?" Fang asked anxiously.

"Faceless. He wears black clothes." Fang, shocked at the description, dropped his jaw. Riley had never seen him look so shaken, and nervousness gripped her as he stared at her with wide eyes.

"Oh, God. How did you..." His expression went blank as his thoughts trailed off. He stood up from the cold ground. "That is impossible," he said, more to himself than to anyone else, "Unless the passageways are much larger than we originally thought."

"What are you talking about?" she asked from on top of her rock.

"The doorways leading from the Shadow World to ours," he said, stopping his pace to explain before quickly losing himself in his thoughts.

She slipped off the rock onto her feet and gave a quick glance around the forest. "So these doorways," she said, "did they just come out of nowhere?"

"Technically, yes," he said hastily. "The hat-man," he added, "where is he now?"

"Uh, I don't know. He shot himself into the shadow creature in Georgia. That was the last time I saw him."

"No, no, no, no!" he yelled. "That's impossible because you are still here. That's impossible unless," he looked at her sharply, "you're a witch."

"She is," Hayden called out. "She's the White Witch," he said. Riley rolled her eyes.

"No, she'd be the Orel not the White," he said. Hayden looked the most confused as he slumped against the tree. Riley could tell that he was thinking about what the man in his head had been telling him for all of the years he had been held kidnapped in the Valley of Hay.

"I don't think she is either," said Fang, watching her closely. "My people would have smelled her as soon as she had crossed into the valley."

"Listen, this doesn't make any sense to me," Riley hushed. "I'm still here because I escaped."

"If what you have told me is the truth, you should be dead right now."

Riley glared at Fang as his eyes flickered from left to right as though he was trying to examine her eyes closely. She wanted out of this maddening situation. "How long until we get out of here?" she hissed. Fang backed away slowly.

"Soon," he replied.

Without saying anything, Fang began to walk downhill toward the beautiful valley that was covered in a light dusting of snow. Riley followed quietly alongside Hayden. The wide, crisp terrain seemed but an illusion as her fingers brushed across the sweat on the back of her neck. She and Hayden stumbled over loose rocks and roots on their trip down. Eventually, they reached the bottom where Hayden slid down the last few feet of hill in a seated position.

Fang took a deep breath and exhaled greatly with a bright smile. He turned to Riley happily. "I have never been this far."

Time suddenly froze. "But you know where we're going, right?" she asked anxiously as Fang looked around the open valley.

"Of course," he said brightly. "It'll just take half a day's walk. We're still pretty far in you know." He gazed up at the sky as though he had no care in the world. "Like I said, the Valley of Hay had to be hidden where no man could accidently find it, but it still had to be easy enough for someone who belongs there to come and go," he added. He turned to view the open valley and appreciated the running water, mountains, and dense patches of evergreen trees.

"Half a day?" she asked, outraged.

"I would much rather travel by flying aircraft once again," he said. "I was flown to Fallsdale to find you, but since you are no longer a friend of those in the Valley of Hay and are currently running off with the Devil," he said, pointing an index at Hayden, "we do not have that option."

"He's not the Devil," Riley interrupted. "Fang, your people were tricked into staying in the Valley of Hay. You were stuck deep in this forest." She raised a finger at him.

"The priests at the time were mistaken," he said. "The boy had powers no one had ever seen before."

"You mean powers like the ones Amanda had?" she shot at Fang, whose nostrils flared.

"But she was a witch, and her powers were definitely not comparable to his. She was caught at a young age and never fully developed like Adelay," he said. He quickly continued before Riley could cut in. "And while witches and warlocks may be able to control their appearances to look attractive, even seconds after looking unfortunate, they cannot live forever. They are not eternal like Hayden is." Fang's eyes were sharp, and his temper was rising.

"Ok," she said, waving her hands in submission. "That still doesn't explain why you guys killed witches when you could have just locked them up like you did with Hayden, eh?" she shot.

"We were told that the Devil could escape his body if he was murdered," he said.

"And the tools he used daily to hurt himself?" she asked, smiling maliciously. "What if he happened to kill himself?"

"Then it would have been him who had done the killing and

he would, therefore, not escape his body into our world but be sent back to Hell."

"The Shadow World," Riley sneered.

"Hell," he snapped. "But he wouldn't kill himself."

"Well, that's a good thing since he's not the Devil." They glared at each other while a dozen sparrows flew from out of the trees and into the sky toward the mountains.

"I suppose," he said finally after an awkward silence.

Fang did not speak for a while following their conversation. They walked down to the stream for a drink before starting to hike alongside the flow of the water. Warblers chirped overhead as the sun hit its highest. As they stopped for another drink from the stream, geese dropped into the water and began to honk but stopped at the sight of Fang's glare. Riley smirked at this display of his animal instinct but kept quiet since she was not yet ready to speak to him.

The walk lasted much longer than a few hours. The sun was lowering in the sky, and everything got colder. Riley's dragging feet were aching against the cold ground, but neither Fang nor Hayden showed any signs of being affected by the sudden changes in the air, so she kept quiet. She yawned and wiped the sleep from her eyes and continued to follow behind Fang.

The stream they were following finally led up to a cave. Fang looked upward to the rising moon. "We should get some rest," he said. Riley desperately wanted to keep walking, but as she slumped against the cave wall, about a dozen feet away from the white noise of the running water, she became completely aware of her exhaustion. Fang made a quick skim through the small cave and reappeared nearly three minutes later. He rested at the cave's mouth and sat facing Riley from the wall opposite her. Hayden sat the closest to the open, freezing air and played with the white snow in his hands. Riley's arms closed tight around the single strapped bag containing the mysterious leather bound book and her eyes clamped shut instantly, and she drifted into sleep.

She knew instantly that she was dreaming. Or was she waking up from a nightmare? She sat up on her comfortable, dark blue couch in the living room. She brushed the blonde bangs from her face and jumped to her feet. A little black fly lunged itself repeatedly at the outside of the window, attempting to get in. She backed away and walked into the main hallway where Peck stood up and stared at her with his head tilted. Peck did nothing but stare while she rushed past him into the kitchen where Parker sat at the table. She was looking at her reflection in a hand mirror. Parker touched a bleeding cut across her cheek, and it healed instantly. For a moment, Parker broke her gaze to smile at Riley, and then she continued her self-admiration. Riley found her way into the bathroom. Hayden stood looking at the mirror above the sink. Black numbers began to spontaneously form on the mirror's surface. They wrote "714" over and over. His eyes lifted up to meet hers in the reflection. She backed away and walked into her messy bedroom. Fang sat next to the window in a hardwood chair which Riley recognized from his cabin in the Valley of Hay. A full moon shone from behind the clouds outside. Fang looked up at her with a sad expression, and she turned around immediately to rush back into the kitchen. Parker still sat at the table, but she was wearing an entirely different outfit.

White Witch?" whispered Hayden's voice at the back of her mind as she stared into Parker's hazelnut eyes. "White Witch?" Hayden's voice whispered again, and Riley woke up to find Hayden sitting by her side.

She could see Fang by the stream with his hands in the water. "White Witch, are you alright?" he asked. Riley looked up to his anxious eyes. "You were shaking. We are still here. Fang is getting you something to drink," he added.

"Hayden," she whispered, "I'm not the White Witch."

Meanwhile

◊ ◊ ◊

Fallsdale was covered with a thin layer of frost. As the woman made her way to the church, her beautiful, long, dark brown hair swayed in the cool wind. She walked on the icy sidewalk wearing jeans and a grey pea coat with a beautiful smile on her face.

The woman's shoes made clicking noises every time she took a step forward. Her brown eyes looked around happily as she drew closer to her destination. She could hear bells erupting from the church, and people piled out into the moonlight. Each member of the crowd was happy to shake hands with and hug the newlywed couple. The people took pictures as the woman with the long, dark hair came closer.

A black limo pulled in front of the wooden doors of the church. The bride and groom along with their bridesmaids and best men happily hopped into the car, and the other guests began to leave for the reception. The woman crossed the street as the limo took off. She reached the doors, grabbed hold of the cold handle, and walked in. The church was warm and inviting. Stained glass paintings hung across the room on both walls. At the front of the sanctuary, the priest knelt to put out candles.

She waited for him to notice her, hoping that he would remember.

She watched him calmly, relishing in the sight of the priest's few moments of happiness. Finally, he turned and saw her through the corner of his eye. The priest did not seem to react as she had expected he would. She pointed to the confessional, and he nodded happily and waved her in. She sat patiently inside the enclosed space and waited for the priest to put out every last candle. She stared through the screen window at a picture that hung on the wall in the other side of the booth.

It was a while before the priest entered the opposite side of the confessional. The woman smiled blissfully while the priest made himself comfortable.

"Forgive me for not making an appointment, Father," said the woman in a calm voice.

"All is forgiven," said the priest through the screen divider. He nodded for her to go on.

The woman smirked at the old man. He did not recognize her. Perhaps it had been too long since he last saw her. She was much younger when his eyes last looked over her face. She took in as much pleasure as she could from this moment before she continued.

"I have sinned," she said. The priest nodded. "I'm afraid I shall again and very soon," she added, emphasizing her last words.

The old man behind the screen listened quietly, still not catching on to her meaning. He turned to face her. "What have you done, my child?" he asked.

She took a moment of silence, pretending that every word she spoke was painful. "I have murdered," she said, fighting back a grin.

The priest sat back in his seat. He stared at the picture on the wall in front of him. "May I ask why you have committed this sin?"

"Of course," she said. "I was forced to."

"I see," he said compassionately. The woman could not help but smile. "And you say you may be forced to commit another murder?"

"No, I will," she said. She could see the priest stir in his seat.

"You *will* be forced?" he asked, his deep voice rising.

She turned and pressed her face against the screen window to get a better look at him. "Do you honestly forget me?" she asked. The priest turned a sickened pale white.

"Should I remember you, miss?" he asked with worried eyes.

"Come on Monsignor," she said, pressing her face harder against the screen. "It's me," she told him with an insane smile. She was finally going to do it. "Adelay Vandarg."

CPSIA information can be obtained at www.ICGtesting.com
Printed in the USA
LVOW080423190512

282367LV00003B/12/P